MW00680548

THE SUNRISE DINER

Best regards,

Also by
Leonard Johnsen

Comes the Blind Fury
and
A Capital Crime

THE SUNRISE DINER

by

Leonard Johnsen

Press-TIGE Publishing
Catskill, New York

Copyrighted 1999 by Leonard Johnsen
ISBN# 1-57532-257-9

All rights reserved. No part of this publication may be reproduced,
stored in a retrieval system, or transmitted in any form or
by any means—electronic, mechanical, photocopy, recording
or any other, except for brief quotations in printed reviews—without
prior permission of the publisher.

For information:

Press-TIGE Publishing
291 Main Street
Catskill, NY 12414
http://presstigebooks.com
Presstige9@aol.com

First Press-TIGE Edition 2000
Cover and book design: Drawing Board Studios

This is a work of fiction. Names, characters, places, and incidents
either are the product of the author's imagination or are used
fictitiously. Any resemblance to actual events or persons, living or
dead is entirely coincidental.

Printed in the United States of America

To Marybeth, Frank, Dylan, Kelly, Conner, Steven, Jack, and, of coarse, the Duker.

Acknowledgment

To my editor, Carol Patton, for her wisdom,
perspective and unlimited patience.

CHAPTER ONE

THE NEWS OF the deaths grabbed this small town by the throat and shook it until it could no longer breathe. Three nights ago, two local kids were found hanged in some sort of weird suicide pact. A community stricken by the enormity of the loss wondered why. Why would two people who had planned to marry later that year kill themselves? By all accounts, they were happy and deeply in love ever since their junior year in high school. It just didn't make sense.

Lou Getz, Mauch Chunk's Chief of Police, received the call at precisely 11:05 p.m. Tom and Ruth Stevens had just returned home when they discovered the gruesome scene, their daughter Mary Jo and future son-in-law Pete Koegel dangling from two ropes draped over a water pipe in the basement. It was grotesque to say the very least. With mouths agape, their lifeless eyes were open wide as though they were witnesses to someone else's death. Blood had caked on their lips and lower jaws and suffused blood had pooled into their lower extremities, distorting them like misshapen water balloons.

The Chief and one of his officers found one chair tipped over at the grisly scene but no suicide note. On Sunday morning after the discovery, he visited briefly with both families and, not surprisingly, neither one could come up with a reason why something like this happened. As far as they knew, the kids were happy, in love and looking forward to their wedding in December.

What was so strange was that Chief Getz had recently read about two teenagers up in New York who were found dead in each other's arms. The coroner concluded that it was a suicide pact and, according to the note they left behind, they did it to spite their parents who vehemently opposed their marriage. But this was a whole lot different. Both sets of parents were as excited as the kids and, unlike the case in New York, Mary Jo was not pregnant. At least, Chief Getz prayed she wasn't.

To make matters even worse, earlier that same evening, a prisoner named Clinton Strock escaped from the Carbon County Jail after striking the warden and walking out the front entrance. Serving an 18-month sentence for assault with intent to ravish, Strock had not been apprehended although the Mauch Chunk Police Department, the Carbon County Sheriff's Department and the Pennsylvania State Police were all involved in the manhunt. Six feet tall, weighing 185 pounds, he was considered extremely powerful and dangerous.

How could these things happen in a quiet Pennsylvania town like Mauch Chunk, a picturesque village nestled in the Lehigh Valley, sandwiched between the mountains and the Lehigh River? Bad things weren't supposed to happen here, a tiny Victorian town steeped in mining, canal and railroad history. Besides, at 60 years of age, Chief Lou Getz didn't need the aggravation.

IT WAS HERE in the extreme western end of Carbon County that anthracite coal was found, as far back as 1791, if one believed the locals. But its most effective use wasn't discovered until 1820 when Josiah White and Erskine Hazard leased the land, then built the Lehigh Canal, a body of water that ran seventy-two miles from White Haven in the upper Lehigh River Valley to Easton on the Delaware River.

One of the men who ran coal-boats on the Lehigh Canal was Asa Packer who later built the Lehigh Valley Railroad, which traveled along 650 miles of track between New York State and the New Jersey seaboard. To this day, The Lehigh Coal and Navigation Company has run the mining operation. But with the increasing importance of oil and other fuels, coal mining towns were losing their prominence. It was readily apparent. More and more miners were being laid off and unemployment was becoming an epidemic, particularly in towns like Mauch Chunk where the impact was devastating. The town's well-kept red-brick terraced Victorian houses had their windows boarded up and clutches of middle-aged men were found idling on the main streets of downtown. No longer was it a magnet for writers, artists and other enterprising folks who would visit just to marvel at its splendor. Now this ailing city — first named Coalville, but later changed to Mauch Chunk, an Indian name for Bear Mountain — was slowly vanishing, just like the hopes and dreams of its citizens.

1953. With the end of the Korean War and General Eisenhower in the White House, I thought things were supposed to get better, groaned Chief Getz.

CHAPTER TWO

"HEY, HAROLD, WHAT'S shaking?

"I don't know, Roy. At my age, I guess just about every-thing, particularly my hands."

With a wave of his arm, Roy Gessler summoned Harold Seward over to his booth. "C'mon over, Harold, sit down here with me and George." Because Roy was always stooped over slightly, an affliction from all those years hunched over in the clefts of the coal mines, Harold only heard Roy's voice, hadn't yet seen the face. When he did, he groaned slightly for Roy was not one of Harold's favorite people.

Harold was heading for the counter to order his usual scrambled egg and dry toast breakfast. However, to avoid a scene, he decided to sit in the booth with the other two. Most mornings, Harold needed two cups of coffee before he even came close to being civil. Roy and George had been in the diner for an hour and a half and were already wired, particularly Roy, who was the most acid-tongued man Harold had ever met. One time, a few months back, Harold declined Roy's invitation and for the next hour, heard Roy's sarcastic barbs, strategically lobbed like grenades so that everyone inside the Sunrise Diner could hear them.

So while Harold preferred to sit by himself, he knew that it was no longer possible. He also knew that these weren't nor-mal times and, considering what had just happened to this town, maybe he could learn a thing or two about the deaths of the kids from Roy, the town's chief gossip. Some folks called him Hedda Hopper Gessler, although never to his face. His ire wasn't worth the brief chuckle.

THE SUNRISE DINER was Mauch Chunk's favorite gather-ing place. From six in the morning to almost eight in the evening, the town folk congregated to gossip and review the events 'de jour'. Over one morning's pour from a steaming pot of coffee, more secret information was exchanged inside this glorified mobile home than one would glean at the FBI briefing room down in the nation's capital. The pop music that blasted from the wall-mounted Seeburg Wall-O-Matic juke boxes — Dwayne Eddy, Kay Starr and Frankie Laine entertained throughout most of the day — assured the confidentiality of anything said.

The diner was built in 1938 by The Jerry O'Mahoney Diner Company of Elizabeth, New Jersey. In 1951, it moved next door to the court house, right across Route 209 from the Jersey Central train depot. Overshadowed by the Asa Packer mansion that sat high above overlooking the Mauch Chunk business district — the eatery sat at the heart of the town.

The legacy of German and Irish immigrants who settled in the region to mine the coal and work the railroad was evident on the menu — homemade pierogies, halupki soup and every version of the potato known to mankind. While it ran four pages, coffee and eggs still ruled. Coffee was served in infinitely refillable cups and eggs were prepared any style — sunnyside up or down, over easy, over well, three-minute, five-minute, wet, dry, poached, boiled, ranchero, western and Denver. They came with sides of toast, chili con carne, beans, grits, oatmeal, bacon, sausage, corned beef hash or steak. Once in a while, someone asked for Mississippi round streak, also known as fried bologna. Everything was homemade and nothing was made from powder like some of the other places not too far away. That was just the way those folks liked their food and why they kept coming back, day in and day out.

MOST OF THE banter revolved around the railroad or the coal mining industry and, very often, it concerned the 'sonofabitches' who controlled the mines — the foremen and the bosses who carried out the policies of the operators. However, for the past few days, there had been only one topic of discussion, the senseless deaths of Pete Koegel and Mary Jo Stevens.

After he had shed his coat, Harold asked, "You guys hear anything more about the hangings?" Due to the temperature that had plummeted overnight, his ruddy complexion seemed more pronounced than usual.

"Naw, nothing new, although I understand that Chief Getz is waiting for the lab results. Can't figure out why. Seems cut and dry if you ask me. Can you think of any reason, George?"

"Nope," George replied as he swiped his palm across his greasy hair that had replaced his gold-colored locks some time ago. "Unless it can tell if the kids were drinking or something." .

George Milosevich was the youngest of the three men. He had retired from the mines seven months ago on disability. Pneumoconiosis, or black lung as they called it in the mining regions, got him like just about every other man who worked for The Lehigh Coal and Navigation Company. With symptoms ranging from sleeplessness, weight loss, coughing and shortness of breath, George had to trek over to the medical facility in Allentown every month for his checkup and lung medication. The bronchodilators helped to expand the air passages and the antibiotics helped prevent infections, but the inhalation therapy was the only treatment that really made him feel better, even if it was only temporary. Of course, this didn't stop him from smoking two packs of Pall Malls every day.

George took a huge drag of his cigarette and didn't pay any attention to the long and deep coughs that quickly followed. His mind was on those kids.

"Still can't believe it happened and to think that they were discovered by her folks. Wonder why they did it? Such a terrible thing. No wonder Ruth's still in the hospital." He paused to released a large cloud of smoke. "The Chief said that the scene was macabre, the two of them just hanging there, eyes popping out the way they were."

Roy waved his hand trying to diffuse the blue cloud of smoke that hovered in front of his face. "Man, how can you smoke those things? You know they're going to kill you. Don't you?"

"I figure it don't make much difference now. The mine killed me a long time ago. Might as well enjoy what little time

I got left." He took another long drag on his Pall Mall, then purposely blew the smoke in Roy's direction. A smile crept across his sallow face.

Roy hissed, "Sonofabitch, can't you blow that God-awful smoke some place else?"

"Yeah, I suppose I could." George grinned as smoke leaked wistfully from his nostrils and floated up toward the ceiling. His yellow teeth looked like kernels of corn.

Roy, looking for support, said, "Doesn't his smoke bother you, Harold?"

"Nope, I'm used to it. I used to work in the copy room at the newspaper. Remember?"

From her station across the counter, Daisy yelled, "Hey, Roy, give George a break. If I had to sit and listen to you rant and rave all day long, I'd chain-smoke too." Her eyes glistened as she laughed.

"Now don't you pay Roy no heed, George," she continued. "You can smoke in here any time you darn well please." Daisy knew that it was just a matter of time before George succumbed to the disease that ravaged men like Misery's hand. Sooner or later, they all did, so why not let the man live out what days he had left in peace.

George threw up his hand and yelled, "Thanks, Daisy, and don't worry about old Roy here. I seldom listen to him anyway. He's so full of it he needs a cork to stop from soiling himself." George laughed, then began to cough. With no sputum to hack up, he would go on for a minute or so before stopping.

DAISY CONNOR WAS a co-owner of the Sunrise Diner. She, along with her half-sister Babs Strohl, bought the place a couple of years back with the insurance money Daisy received after her husband died in that terrible mine collapse. Five men were buried for nearly twenty-three hours before rescuers got to them. There was only one survivor and he ended up in the state mental ward. Apparently, something snapped inside his head about the time the main header beam snapped and interred the six miners. That all happened three years ago and, to this day, Daisy cringes any time the name The Lehigh Coal and Navigation Company was brought up in the conversation. *Heartless bastards. Not one of the bosses showed up for his funeral,* she often thought.

Anyway, Daisy and Babs fixed up the Sunrise Diner real nice. They redid the outside, replaced the worn brown stools and booths inside, and hired a decent fry cook, an old sailor who just happened to wander in one afternoon. Ever since then, the place had turned a small profit.

Aside from weekend mornings, the two owners alternated their time at the diner. It was easy to tell the two apart. Daisy's blonde hair was pulled up into a tight bun, which provided a handy place for her to park the pencil she needed to write down the food orders. Overweight — there were times when it appeared she was ready to pop out of her pink-striped waitress uniform — she was the official tester of the french fries as soon as the chef took them out of the hot oil.

Babs kept her brown hair short. She prided herself on the fact that she didn't need a pencil and could rely on her remarkable memory. She called both men and women 'hon', always snapped her stick of Juicy Fruit to the beat of the music, and let any customer know by way of a sour look if the tip was small.

Both women were in their mid-forties, hard-working and, considering the clientele, patient as saints. At times, George thought he had a thing for Babs, but at his age, he wasn't exactly sure what that *thing* was.

As Kelly, the diner's part-time waitress, poured a second cup of forty-weight for the boys, Officer Randy Furey burst through the front glass door.

"Hey, Randy, take it easy on the door," Daisy shouted.

Daisy had an unusually loud voice. Roy thought it might have something to do with her husband who had been hard of hearing for the last ten years of his life, thanks to working in the mines. She had gotten used to screaming for his benefit.

"Oh, sorry, Miss Daisy. It's just that it's getting a little chilly out there. Couldn't wait to get inside." Randy removed his hat and slapped it against his thigh. He then eyeballed the booth and said, "Howya doing, fellas?"

Randy was one of Mauch Chunk's finest, had been for nearly a year. From nearby Hazelton, he had left for Penn State after high school with grandiose plans of being a police chief for some big city. He flunked out his first year, yet somehow managed to get an associates degree from the local community college.

A private with the Army's 82nd Airborne outside of Fayetteville, he later volunteered for the Special Forces Group that also trained down in Fort Bragg. After that stint, he returned home, settled in Mauch Chunk, then joined the police department, a crack fighting force of three men and one woman dispatcher, three patrol cars and the old county jail up on Broadway that housed the malcontent, occasional drunk or vagrant.

Randy was a big strapping kid with a mean streak a mile long. With reddish-brown hair and a square jaw, he looked a little like the cartoon character, Joe Palooka. A good day for him was chasing speeders out on Route 903, pulling them over, then sauntering up to the driver's side window in his nicely pressed uniform, spit shined boots and aviator sunglasses, to issue the summons. There was no use trying to reason with the boy, for he had no time for it. Randy really liked being the intimidator.

"Anything further on the hangings?" asked Roy nonchalantly. He didn't look at Randy and kept his eyes focused on his stained coffee cup. He thought by acting indifferently, Randy would be more willing to confide in him and share all the gruesome details.

Randy hesitated for a moment before answering. "Nope, nothing yet." Uncomfortable pauses were pretty normal when anyone tried to hold a conversation with him.

Roy continued, "It's a good thing for you that you were off duty on Saturday. Pretty awful scene, as I hear it. Where were you, anyway?"

Daisy piped in, "That's none of your business, Roy. Hey, Randy, you know you don't have to answer to him, don't you?" She laughed then returned to what she was doing.

"That's all right, Miss Daisy," Randy laughed unconvincingly. "I went to the Penn State game."

"Hell of a game, huh?" Roy remarked.

"Yes, sir, it surely was." Randy then turned toward the counter and asked Daisy for three coffees to go, two black and one with cream, no sugar.

As Daisy hollered back that they would be right up, Roy raised his arm and asked, "Hey, Randy, who won, anyway? State?"

"Oh, uh, I'm not sure. We left before it was over." He reached into his pocket for some change and slapped it on the counter as Daisy appeared with his order. As he snatched up the paperbag, he thanked Daisy, tipped his hat and headed out the door.

At that point, Roy turned to his companions and whispered, "I know for a fact that game was a goddamn blowout, 60 something to 3. Most likely, the kid was drinking. It's a wonder he made it back here alive. Between being stupid, drunk and driving that old junk of his, I'm surprised he didn't have to be pried him out of his car with a shoe horn."

"Oh, I suppose you never took a drink in your life, huh?" Harold finally amassed the courage to open his mouth.

"Well I'll tell you one thing, smart ass," Roy snarled, "I never drink and drive."

"That's because you can't find your car when you're drunk," George teased. Everybody in the place exploded with laughter. Everybody except Roy Gessler. He had just gotten a dose of his own medicine and he didn't like the way it tasted.

Chapter Three

HARRY ARNETT, THE Carbon County Coroner, called Chief Lou Getz first thing Wednesday morning. He had completed the autopsies and the two reports were being typed as they spoke. But since he had found an irregularity, he thought that the Chief should be aware of it a soon as possible.

"What is it, Harry? Did you find something?"

"Yeah, we sure did. We found a contusion on the base of each of their necks. The bruises and edema are consistent with a blow to the back of the head with a heavy object."

"Christ, Harry, what are you saying?"

"I'm saying that the force of this blow was enough to render them both unconscious."

"Are you telling me that someone else strung them up? He didn't wait for Arnett's reply. "Damnit, Harry, do you know what this means? If you're right, we've got a murderer running around loose in Carbon County."

"I can't be a hundred percent sure, Lou, but I don't think you can rule it out either. Hey, when we opened them up, we found macaroni and cheese in their stomachs, for God's sake. Does that sound like something they'd do just prior to killing themselves, sit down to dinner?"

"No, I guess not." The Chief rubbed his eyes, trying to put this new information into perspective. "Couldn't those marks be from the rope?" asked the Chief. "I mean, wouldn't the rope cause the same kind of bruising?"

Harry explained that during a hanging, very little pressure was exerted by the rope on the back of the neck, near the knot. In fact, the rope hardly touched the back of the neck because a natural gap occurred when the weight of the body pulled on the noose. Almost all of the pressure was in the front of the throat, right underneath the chin.

"Then what do you think killed them? Strangulation or the blows to the neck?"

"My guess it was asphyxiation due to strangulation caused by the rope." His voice trailed off.

The Chief reached for his chair. *Pete and Mary Jo murdered?* He didn't know what to say let alone think. He had been Chief of Police in this town for a number of years and the worst thing that ever happened was when Mrs. McCreary's old hound broke its leg in a hit and run car accident. Even then, everybody knew it was old man Tucker who was too proud to wear his driving glasses.

"And, Lou, I didn't find any hair or tissue samples under their fingernails and there were no other marks or bruises that would indicate that a scuffle took place."

The Chief remained silent. "Lou? Hello? Are you still there?"

"Yeah, Harry, I'm here." Lou sounded like he was a million miles away.

"Sorry I don't have better news. I'll have Ned drive over the autopsy report later today." The line went dead before Getz could wish Harry success in the upcoming elections. Harry was running for County Treasurer. *From chief medical examiner to chief financial examiner,* mused the Chief. *Quite a stretch.*

For quite a while Chief Getz sat in his worn out leather chair before hanging up the receiver. *Pete and Mary Jo murdered? Why? Who would want to kill two nice kids?* the Chief asked himself. *And why didn't I think to dust the Stevens' basement for prints? It's probably too late for that. The area is contaminated by now. God, I hope Harry's wrong.*

The Chief stood up and poked his head out the door of his tiny office. "Hey, Billy, get in here."

Billy Chalk was 38 years old and a ten-year veteran of the Mauch Chunk Police Department. He married his high school sweetheart, soon had two children — a boy and a girl — and he and the family attended St. Marks Episcopal Church religiously. While not as powerful or as daring as Randy Furey, he still was the cop that the Chief relied upon whenever something had to be done and done correctly. Flat feet kept him out of Korea. Now he was a flat foot. Life is full of twists and turns.

Chalk strolled into the office and the Chief closed the door. "Listen, Billy, I'm going tell you something and I want it to stay in this room. I just got off the horn with the coroner.

To make a long story short, he thinks that Mary Jo and Pete might've been murdered."

"*Murdered?*" Chalk shouted. He looked like he had just been slapped in the face.

The Chief placed his index finger to his lips. "Shush, I don't want Randy to hear. You know how he likes to shoot off his mouth. If he hears about this, the whole goddamn town will know. We've got to keep this quiet, at least for the time being."

The Chief explained that Arnett found bruises on the backs of their necks, like they might have been struck by someone or something and he thought that they could have been unconscious when they were strung up.

"So somebody tried to make it look like a suicide. But why?"

"I haven't a clue."

The Chief sat down and looked up at Chalk with a rueful expression. He told Billy that they had another problem. They never dusted the place for fingerprints or, for that matter, collected any other trace evidence.

"Now, this is what I need you to do. Run over to the Stevens' place and search the basement for any clues. Dust for prints and look for anything else that might help us in our investigation. Leave no stone unturned." The Chief knew that last comment sounded trite.

"I doubt we'll find anything, Chief."

"I know, but it's worth a shot. Another thing, don't let Tom Stevens know what you're doing. Just tell him that I sent you back over to review the scene. Tell him it's routine."

"Hey, Chief, if the coroner's right, who do you think did it?"

Getz shook his head. "I don't have the foggiest, Billy. Right now, our only suspect is Clinton Strock, the escapee, but for the life of me, I can't figure out why he'd do such a thing." The Chief had turned and was staring out the window as Chalk left the office. His face was expressionless.

AT 10:15, MARGARET Wenzel called the Mauch Chunk Police Station in a panic. "Lou, you'd better get out here right

away. Somebody's over by the Switchback railroad bed. I can see him from my front door. He may be that guy you're looking for, the guy who escaped from the jail Saturday night. He's acting sneaky-like, skulking around like a wounded animal. Can't explain it. You'd better get over here and take a look-see for yourself." She stopped when she ran out of breath.

Margaret was one of three people who lived by the lake, just a little ways out on Broadway. While desolate enough for those who yearned for peace and quiet, the lake and the wooded area around it were but a stone's throw from civilization back in Mauch Chunk proper. Margaret Wenzel had lost her husband ten years ago to Black Lung and ever since, she had sort of checked out from the rest of society.

Lou told Margaret to lock all her doors and windows. There was no telling what this stranger would do if he spotted her. "Can you see him from where you are?"

"Yeah, sort of. I can't see him right at the moment, but I know he's there just the same."

"Keep an eye on him and, if you see him moving away, call Annie, my dispatcher. She'll relay any message to us on the two-way radio. We'll be there in ten minutes."

"Thanks, Lou. Please get out here as soon as you can."

Chief Getz hung up the phone and told Randy to grab two rifles and two hundred rounds of ammo from the arsenal in the weapons room. As Randy ran toward the rear of the building, Chief Getz called the County Sheriff's Department and told them about the sighting. They confirmed that they would relay the information on to the State Police barracks over in Lehighton and all three law enforcement bodies would reconnoiter at 11:15 at the boathouse out at Mauch Chunk Lake. Nobody was to do anything until the State Police arrived. As with most investigations of that nature, the state had taken control of the manhunt for the escaped prisoner Clinton Strock. They didn't need some small town police chief or county sheriff screwing things up.

After he filled in his dispatcher, Chief Getz and Patrolmen Furey hopped into one of the two Plymouths parked outside. With one hundred horsepower and a 7.1 to 1 compression ratio, it wouldn't take them very long to get out to the rail bed.

CHAPTER FOUR

CARBON COUNTY WAS the home of the first railroad in America that was built on any large scale. The Switchback railroad, as it came to be known in its heyday, was built in 1827 by the founders of the Lehigh Coal and Navigation Company. Originally designed to carry coal, the Switchback gravity railroad ran for nine miles from the Great Mine of Summit Hill down the mountain and through the valley of the Mauch Chunk Creek to a transfer point on the Lehigh Canal at Mauch Chunk. From there, the coal was loaded onto canal boats and shipped to the growing eastern cities of Philadelphia and New York. It was called a gravity railroad because the coal-cars were hitched together outside the mine and the brakeman rode the powerless train down the mountain at breakneck speeds, often reaching fifty miles per hour. Mules then pulled the empty cars nine miles back up the hill. While the descent took only thirty-five minutes, the return trip took nearly three hours.

Later, the enterprising owners recognized another market for their railroad. In between coal trains, the promoters would send trains full of tourists plummeting down the mountainside on a high-speed, thrill-ride, the world's first roller coaster. People came from all over to experience the exhilaration of the ride.

While the railroad was no longer in operation — now just a vast hillside sloping off to one side covered with weeded-over crushed concrete and rusty cables — the path of the railroad had remained intact and served as a hiking and biking trail out by the lake, not far from Margaret Wenzel's property.

CLINTON STROCK, THE escaped convict from the Carbon County Jail, didn't enjoy being hunted like an animal by the police or by anyone else, for that matter. He couldn't figure out how he'd gotten himself into such a fix. "All I did was punch the guy," he kept telling the judge, ignoring the fact that the assault occurred while he was trying to rob the man's jewelry store. "It's not like I shot him or anything."

But the judge saw things differently and sentenced him to eighteen months for assault with intent to ravish. To this day, Strock still didn't have a clue as to what "ravish" meant.

After the trial, the county transported him over to the Carbon County Jail in Mauch Chunk. Strock felt that his punishment was above and beyond what any civilized human being should have to endure.

The Carbon County Jail was a medieval-like fortress, a gray stone citadel built in 1869. Inside, twenty-four cells lined the central corridor in two tiers. Sixteen more could be found in the dank dungeon, some with marks of shackles. The main stone walls were three feet thick. The heat was coal generated and not very effective, especially at this time of year. The little bit of warmth that made its way up from the belly of the jail through the tiny holes in the concrete floors was barely enough heat to keep any normal man alive. The prisoners had only two opportunities each day to relieve themselves and thirty minutes a day for exercise in an outdoor recreational area that was surrounded by a twenty-foot stone wall. This was hardly humane treatment, especially for a man like Clinton Strock who should not have been incarcerated in the first place. *Hell, if I hadn't been laid off at the coal mine, I wouldn't have had to steal anything,* Strock thought. *Society made me commit that crime. What I did sure wasn't bad enough to lock me up in that goddamned Cell Seventeen like a fucking dog. They'll pay for it. They can't do this to Clinton Strock.*

Well lock him up they did and it didn't take him very long to take matters into his own hands. On Saturday night, October 24th, Strock asked for and was granted a meeting with Warden McBride. After a very brief and private conference in his office, he struck the warden in the face, grabbed his keys and went AWOL.

For more than three days, Clinton Strock had been sneaking around the Mauch Chunk area, stealing food from window sills and milk from back stoops and sleeping in tool sheds or in whatever else he could find that offered protection from the ice cold October evenings. Since he was a rather large man, sneaking around was hard on him. A couple of times he even wished he was back in that dank cell and out of the bone-chilling wind.

Today, he was over by the railroad tracks, huddled under the burnt orange and crimson leaves next to an old tree trunk — Strock didn't know that the Switchback trains that once rode these rails stopped operating a long time ago, sometime back in the 1930's.

The smell of the fallen leaves reminded him of his childhood back in Bath when they used to celebrate the annual pageantry of color by burning the leaves he and his father had raked earlier. That was long before his father lay dying in that hospital with a respirator stuck up his nose. Black lung ended up killing him at the age of 53. His father had worked down in the mines for over twenty-five years. *Twenty-five years for what?* he asked himself. *So his lungs could fill with black dust, poison that killed him and his dreams?*

Strock's long-range plans were tenuous at best. Since he wasn't from this area originally, he had no idea how to escape on the county roads. He was afraid to use the main highways for fear he would run smack into the law, so he decided to wait for the next train that just didn't seem to want to come. It had now been a day and a half and he hadn't heard even the hint of a train whistle much less the roar of a diesel engine.

According to the bright orange sun that hovered overhead, it was nearly twelve when he first spotted two siren-less State Police cars cruising on the main road that ran along the lake. These vehicles were followed by two or three other official-looking cars with different markings. Obviously, he'd been spotted by someone. It didn't matter who, he just had to get out of there and fast. *Probably that old lady across the highway,* he thought as he turned and ran for his life.

Strock got on all fours and clawed his way up the steep hill. Steam huffed from his mouth as he slipped on the oily leaves still wet from the previous night's brief downpour. When he grabbed for a low tree branch, it broke off and Strock slid back to the spot where he had first begun. He tried again, this time with more success. After scratching and scraping, he finally managed to reach the top of the hill overlooking the lake. He rolled over on his back and onto the other side. He was panting heavily. Though the physical exertion made it feel as though his lungs might explode, he craved a cigarette, nonetheless.

He carefully poked his head back over and saw six or seven uniformed men huddled together, apparently concocting some sort of strategy. Like a turtle, Strock slowly retracted his head, took a deep breath, stood up and ran like the dickens down the other side of the hill. Twice he fell and rolled head over heels out of control. Fortunately, he didn't break an arm or a leg. He righted himself again, then continued the precarious trek down the mountainside. After descending nearly fifteen hundred feet, he finally reached the bottom where he sat and rested again. Puffs of white smoke chugged from his mouth.

Had he gotten out of harm's way? *No*, he thought. He had to keep going even though his lungs had seized like an engine without oil. He knew if the cops looked closely, they would see his claw marks along the hillside and be able to track his muddy footprints. He decided to run for another twenty minutes and then find some place to hide. If they apprehended him after all that, more power to them. He deserved his fate.

It was around three in the afternoon when Lieutenant Arthur Champion of the State Police called off the manhunt. "No telling where he is now, fellas. I say we pack it in. There'll be other leads, you can bet on it. We'll nab him, it just won't be today. And next time, we'll bring the dogs."

As a despondent Chief Getz returned alone in his police vehicle, he felt a heaviness in his heart. He realized for the first time that if the Coroner's suspicions were correct, Clinton Strock was his only suspect in the deaths of Mary Jo Stevens and Pete Koegel and he was still on the loose.

Back at headquarters, the Chief reviewed the autopsy reports that Harry Arnett had sent over earlier, then called Billy into his office. He closed the door.

"You find anything up at the Stevens' place?"

"You're not going to like it, Chief." He hesitated momentarily before continuing. "The only prints I found on the chair were yours and mine. Looks like it had been wiped clean."

"Maybe the Stevens cleaned things up after we left," responded the Chief.

"No, not according to Tom. He said they haven't gone down to the basement since it happened, maybe never will."

The Chief then sank down into his old chair behind his desk, appearing somewhat defeated.

"Even the basement door knob was clean and the water pipe used to tie the rope to," added Billy. "My guess is that someone wiped everything down before we got there. I think Harry might be right. Those kids didn't commit suicide. They were murdered."

The Chief scratched his chin and said, "Yeah, looks that way. If they'd killed themselves, there'd be prints all over the place. And we can't forget the macaroni and cheese dinner they ate. What about the banister?"

"There were smudged prints, just no clean ones. I'd say that whoever committed the crime came through the basement door, never used the cellar stairs. Both the interior and exterior door knobs were clean as a whistle."

"Anything else?"

Billy just shook his head, feeling like he had somehow failed and disappointed the Chief.

Considering the lateness of the hour, the Chief decided to have a talk with Tom Stevens sometime tomorrow after the funeral. Tom had been through enough without Lou hitting him with news that his daughter and future son-in-law were possibly murdered. After that, he would talk with the Koegel's. In the meantime, he asked Billy to nose around, talk to some of the neighbors. Maybe one of them spotted something unusual that night.

Chalk looked incredulous, then said curtly, "You want me to go up there tonight, Chief?" He looked upset. "Can't Randy cover it?"

"Sorry, Billy, he's got that damn meeting over in Jewett."

"That's near thirty miles from here. What do they do over there, anyway?"

"Beats me, Billy." The Chief removed his hat and scratched an imaginary itch. Other than arranging the annual St. Patrick's Day parade, the Chief really didn't know what the Ancient Order of Hibernians did.

THE ANCIENT ORDER OF HIBERNIAN'S low-profile was a far cry from its past activities. Back in the 1870's, when it was a secret society, some members were accused of harassing non-

Irish miners competing for the jobs, as well as the foremen and mine bosses who carried out the policies of the operators of the local mine fields. Fact is, five of their members were executed right there in Mauch Chunk for the murders of two mine superintendents.

BILLY CHALK WAS halfway out the door when he stopped and turned back toward the Chief who sat at his desk, staring vacantly out the window. Feeling remorseful for snapping at the Chief, he asked, "What are you doing tonight, Chief? You heading home soon?"

"Naw, I've got some paperwork to take care of first. Then I'll probably watch a little television. Perry Como's on. Oh, and I bought one of them new Swanson TV dinners over at the market. According to Herb Nelson, they're being test marketed here in Pennsylvania. Thought I'd give one a try."

"TV dinner, huh? Let me know how it is. The missus might be interested particularly on a night when there's a school board meeting." Chalk began to leave but stopped yet again.

"You know something, Chief? I was thinking that Tom Stevens might even be a little relieved when he finds out that Mary Jo didn't commit suicide. A kid's suicide must be a tough thing for a parent to handle, all the unanswered questions, the guilt and everything."

"Yeah, the fact that they've outlived their child. It must be awful." The Chief again turned toward the window and gazed out upon the evening lights. His thoughts were miles away.

"Chief, one more thing." When the Chief swiveled around in his old chair, it made a terrible squeak. "I didn't see any signs of a break-in. The basement door hadn't been jimmied and there was no broken glass. Do you think the kids might have known their assailant?"

"Hell, Billy, I don't know. That's why I need you to go up there tonight, nose around, see what you can find."

Alone in his office, Chief Getz laced his hands behind his head and put his feet up on the desk. He heard the shrill sound of the train whistle from the depot across the street. Because of the conversation he had just had with Billy, he wished he was on that train, heading as far away from Mauch Chunk as he could possibly get. The further away the better. He hadn't always felt this way, though. Before his wife died, he had sought solace in her arms. That seemed like such a long time ago, when things were so much simpler. She was so beautiful and they were very much in love. He was an athletic man with a full head of hair and a square jaw. He always thought his head a bit too large, but she didn't care, just attributed it to his Slavic heritage. "I wouldn't trade you in for anyone," she would chuckle, "except maybe Clark Gable." Lou smiled to himself.

IT WAS LATE afternoon when Clinton Strock exhumed himself from his makeshift grave that lay between two fallen trees. He brushed himself off, turned up the collar of his khaki shirt to buffer his neck against the cold wind and began his trek back. It was bitterly cold. If he could have felt them, he was almost positive that the muscles in his legs would have ached like the dickens.

During a good part of the evening, Strock retraced his steps back to the lake. He was pretty sure the authorities wouldn't look for him there. More than likely, they would figure he was heading west, away from Carbon County. At one point, he came across a duck blind and found a half quart of Wild Turkey covered in cloth neatly stowed under some empty cartridge boxes. After pouring the whiskey down his parched throat, he heaved the empty bottle against a nearby tree and watched it shatter into a thousand pieces. Then he threw up. The pain in his throat was so excruciating that he had to shovel snow into his mouth to cool the flames.

Even with shaky hands, he managed to snap the lock on Margaret Wenzel's old basement window like a three-week old chicken bone and, despite the creaky hinges, slid through the small opening without making a sound. Inside, Strock stood in pitch darkness for a moment to get his bearings, reeling slightly from the remnants of the liquor. The only illumination came from the sliver of light that sneaked beneath the basement door and wiggled it's way halfway down the cellar stairs like a yellow Slinky. The heat from the old cast-iron furnace was the first warmth he had felt since his last trip to the toilet back at the jail in Mauch Chunk. Although the toilet facilities were something out of the Dark Ages, the bowls sat directly above the heating plant located one floor below. Strock closed his weary eyes and nestled up to the boiler like a cat on its owner's lap. Within minutes, he was sound asleep, oblivious to the fires that raged all around him.

RANDY ARRIVED IN Jewett a little after eight. It was a clear night and he had made good time over the winding roads that led north out of Mauch Chunk. He pulled into the parking lot and sidled up to one of the railroad ties in front of the small wood-frame lodge. He purposely parked next to a brand new Chrysler, the blue one with the souped-up 235-hp Firepower V-8 engine. Before he cut the ignition, he reached down and grabbed the half-empty bottle of whiskey he had tucked under the passenger seat. He first looked to his left, then to his right. When all was clear, he raised the bottle to his lips and took one last swig. Although the whiskey warmed his insides, he shivered nonetheless for it was a cold October night and the Kaiser's cheap heater didn't work very well. He then replaced the fifth underneath the seat and popped a stick of Wrigley spearmint into his mouth as he stepped out of the car.

The first person Randy spotted when he entered the lodge was Brendan Conley who stood among a group of older members in the front of the hall. Conley was glad to see him since he wasn't sure whether Randy had to pull duty that night or not.

Randy and Brendan had served together in the Special Forces down in Fort Bragg and, after a rough beginning, became good friends. Like Randy, Brendan was a big, strapping kid with freckles and a shock of reddish-brown hair that looked as though it had never been combed. He was a locksmith by trade and lived in a dilapidated boarding house just outside of Wilkes-Barre.

Brendan beckoned Randy over with a sweep of his arm and, as they shook hands, each quietly muttered "Here's my mark of innocence." Only they knew what it meant.

Randy and Brendan were the newest members of the lodge. While they knew a couple of the other members by name, the main reason they'd been inducted was because they were the sons of two members who had both died within two years of each other. Certainly, neither Randy or Brendan had done anything on their own to warrant membership consideration. Because of that, Randy and Brendan knew they would have to go out of their way to get noticed by the senior members of Division No. 3 of the Ancient Order of Hibernians.

THE ANCIENT ORDER of Hibernians was a Catholic, Irish-American fraternal organization founded in New York City in 1836. The Order could be traced back to a parent organization that existed in Ireland for over three hundred years. It evolved from a need in the 1600's to protect the lives of priests who risked immediate death to keep the Catholic faith alive in occupied Ireland after the reign of England's King Henry VIII. After England implemented its Penal Laws in Ireland, various secret social groups were formed across the land. These groups worked to aid and comfort the people by whatever means available.

Similarly, the Ancient Order of Hibernians in America was founded to protect the clergy and church property from the "Know Nothings" and their followers. At the same time, the vast influx of Irish immigrants fleeing famine in Ireland in the late 1840's prompted a growth of various social societies here. Active across the United States, the Order aided the newly arrived Irish culture and addressed economic issues and human rights. In the coal mining area of eastern Pennsylvania, the Irish mine workers and their welfare were constant topics discussed at the monthly meetings.

FEIGNING INTEREST, RANDY and Brendan quietly sat through the meeting, a difficult task considering both were slightly inebriated. They cringed when the subject of the St. Patrick's Day parade was brought up before the membership. *Who gives a shit about a fucking parade,* they both thought. *We*

only care about the fate of the Irish workers. Along with the others, they applauded loudly when the president of the division chastised the mine owners and bosses for the unsafe conditions down in the mines and their unfair hiring practices. The membership cheered, too, when it was announced that the national board of the AOH was sending a delegation to Washington to speak with officials of the Eisenhower administration. *Finally, something worthwhile is happening,* they thought.

When the meeting finally adjourned, sometime around nine-thirty, Randy and Brendan left the hall immediately and got into Randy's old Kaiser. Most of the others remained inside while members of the entertainment committee uncovered several bottles of liquor that had been hidden under an old bed sheet. This was usually how most meetings ended, unless, of course, the president deemed the weather too inclement and ordered everyone home to their wives and children. That evening, however, men with names like Pat, Duffy, Mike and Fitz congregated around the makeshift bar and drank to the Ancient Order of Hibernians. Blessedly, God was again watching over them, for the night was crystal clear.

Randy reached down and grabbed the half-empty bottle of Jack Daniels, took a mighty swig, then handed it to Brendan who did the same. They talked and argued for almost an hour before Brendan drove off, the tires of his new Chrysler leaving a cloud of dust in their wake. As the pebbles flew against Randy's hubcaps, an odd rat-a-tat resonated into the crisp air. He took one more swallow, then rolled down the window to clear his head.

Danny Boy bellowed from inside, a sure sign that the others would soon be leaving. He raised the collar of his coat against the bitter cold and turned the ignition key. *Thank God it started,* Randy thought. *If we want to make an impression with these people, they can't see us drunk.*

He nosed his automobile out onto the highway, then began the long trek south. It was another quarter of a mile before he pulled out the headlight knob.

CHAPTER FIVE

"HEY, ROY, YOU chipped in your five cents yet?"

"Whaddaya talking about, George? What five cents?" The meeting of the Sunrise Diner curmudgeons had officially begun.

"Hell, I thought you would've heard by now. The Industrial Association of Mauch Chunk is trying to collect five cents a week from each resident for the industrial and scenic development of the town." George was amazed that he actually knew something that Roy didn't.

Placing his cup into the coffee-soaked saucer, Roy lectured, "Hell, George, a nickel's nothing more than a fly on an elephant's ass. It's going to take a whole lot more than five cents a week to clean up this dump. Even if they collect the money, they'll probably piss it away anyhow. I've seen it all before and I'm sure I'll see it again."

At this point, George didn't even want to be Roy's friend. He was tired of his constant complaining. He tapped out a Pall Mall and lit up behind a plume of yellow flame. As he turned slightly in his seat, he took a deep drag and watched as the smoke billowed up toward the ceiling vent.

Just as Roy asked George what was the matter, Randy barged through the front door.

"Morning, Roy, George. Man, I tell you, it's cold out there. It almost feels like snow." Both men shivered as the cold air made it's way to their booth and smacked them like a thrown snowball.

"How's it going, Randy? Understand you and the others almost caught the escaped prisoner yesterday." Roy still refused to look the officer squarely in the eye.

"Yeah, I guess." Randy was hung over, hadn't had a chance to clear out the cobwebs yet. The two aspirin tablets he had taken earlier hadn't yet kicked in.

As he rubbed the bridge of his nose with his fingers, Randy continued. "Old lady Wenzel thought she might have seen him out by the old Switchback. We didn't find anything though. It was probably just a deer." He mounted the stool near the register and began tapping his fingers on the counter.

"Anything more on the hangings, son?"

Still hurting, Randy rubbed his forehead with the palm of his hand and replied, "Haven't heard anything, Roy, and I don't expect to. In my book, a hanging's a hanging. It don't take no Einstein to figure it out."

Randy was obviously annoyed. Finally, when Babs was free, he ordered four coffees, picked up the bag, then exited the diner just as Harold was entering.

Like the day before, Roy motioned Harold over with a sweep of his arm. He slid in next to George, then let out a loud sigh.

As he lit up yet another Pall Mall, George Milosevich asked, "Are either of you guys attending the funeral?"

Roy responded, "Naw, really didn't know them that well, only met them a couple of times. Seemed like snotty kids to me. Anyway, I hate funerals. There's only one funeral I'll be attending."

"And it can't come soon enough," George whispered under his breath. "What about you, Harold?" Harold nodded.

With no use for segue, Roy said, "You guys hear about Timmy Moran? He put his house on the market, moving his family out to Carlisle."

Harold placed his cup back on the saucer, then responded, "Yeah, lots of luck. John Murdoch's been trying to unload his place for nearly six months. No takers."

"What's going on, anyway? George asked, rather concerned. "Why's everybody's being laid off all of a sudden?"

Roy furrowed his brow, then explained that if George had been paying attention, he would have known that it had been going on for almost five years. A couple of guys here, a couple there. It was little wonder. The coal production in that part of Pennsylvania was half what it was back in the forties. And because of all the modern equipment, they didn't need to hire as many miners. Roy said that a worker today could mine twice what he mined ten years ago.

"The real problem is nobody uses anthracite anymore, not with all that cheap natural gas they're pumping in," added Harold. "Hard coal's becoming a thing of the past."

Roy cut in, "You're wrong, Harold. The real problem is that those bastards haven't lifted one finger to help these poor guys. The workers live in uncertainty while the bosses live in the lap of luxury over there on millionaires' row. It's a damn shame."

"I thought the unions were supposed to protect the workers like you and me," George asked as he tapped out another cigarette.

"Didn't help us much now, did they, George?"

George looked down at his coffee cup and let the smoke massage his face. He looked like he was on fire.

BOTH ROY AND George had worked up in the Great Mine at Summit Hill since they were kids. Roy was the heavier of the two and had short-cropped gray hair. He always had the look of someone who knew something others didn't. On the other hand, George, who was five years Roy's junior, was slight of build, mostly due to Black Lung, and looked much older than his years. His hair was long and ratty and seemed as though it was still clogged with that same coal dust. Although the disease had ravaged his body, he always had a twinkle in his eye, unlike Roy, who usually looked as though he had just smelled something rancid.

George was the more upbeat of the pair and certainly better liked than Roy, a man who had the unique knack of turning someone off almost the moment he met them. Why they had become friends was a mystery. Perhaps the real question was why they remained friends.

In contrast, Harold never had to toil down in the mine shafts, not even for a day. After college, he went to work for the Mauch Chunk Times-News as a copy boy and, in time, worked his way up to lead reporter. His only connection to the coal mines were his scathing articles about the unfair practices by the owners and bosses. His series of articles on automation that had helped eliminate thousands of jobs in the entire

Carbon County coal region was so insightful that it was later reprinted in The New York Times. Harold endeared himself with the townsfolk after that and sort of became a celebrity. Still, his jaunty mien and quick wit could not hide the ashen skin and hollow eyes, a consequence of too many hours locked away in the press room and not enough time out in the glorious Pennsylvania air.

"THINGS SHOULD IMPROVE now that Ike's in the White House," Roy said knowingly. "Remember Old Harry, he never took shit from those union bosses. Ike won't either. Remember when Truman threatened to bring in the army to run the railroads? Man, Truman was one tough sonofabitch."

"Yeah, but he was fair," chimed George. "When the unions started acting up, old Harry put up his hand up to stop them, then later tried to veto the Taft-Hartley Act. Not many presidents would've done that particularly at a time when the country felt that the unions had grown too powerful.

"Don't kid yourself, Roy, Eisenhower's no slouch either. Remember, he practically defeated the whole goddamn German army by himself. He's not about to let John L. Lewis or anybody else, for that matter, run roughshod over him. Ike says he wants to amend the Act, repeal some of the pro-management issues. And watch out for this Nixon guy. I understand he's a bulldog."

"You can say what you want but mark my words, Ike's no Harry Truman. Hey, Babs, how about another cup of joe?"

Harold stretched his arms out wide and yawned heavily. As he tried to rid himself of last night's sleep, his eyes hit upon the mirrored ceiling. He recoiled when he saw the reflection, a weathered old man staring right back down at him. He wondered why the mirror was installed up there. Was it to give the appearance that the diner was bigger than it actually was? And why was the counter gray, the tables pinkish, the black-and-white tiles checkered and the Naugahyde on the metal stools turquoise? Most of all, what were those pierogi things Daisy and Babs had on the menu? Harold would never eat anything called a *pierogi*.

As George excused himself to go to the men's room, Roy commented, "Geez, George, you piss more than a race horse. If those cigarettes don't kill you first, then you're probably going to die of dehydration. Maybe you should knock off the coffee and just eat bread." Roy chuckled as George headed toward the back with a glum look on his face.

After a few minutes George returned to the booth. As Babs arrived with a fresh pot of coffee, George wiped off a wet spot on the front of his khaki trousers with a paper towel.

"Geez, can't you do that inside the crapper, George?" sniped Roy.

"Damnit, Roy, it's water from the faucet," George barked, looking a bit embarrassed.

"Yeah, sure, and I'm the King of Siam. It's piss and you know darned well it is."

Babs shushed Roy and warned him about talking trash in the diner.

"Okay, okay, Babs, don't get your panties in a bind." As Babs recoiled, George began a coughing jag that lasted a full minute. When he finished, he wiped his mouth with a napkin, checked it for blood — there was none — then lit up another Pall Mall. His eyes were clouded with tears.

Babs thought about giving Roy a tongue-lashing but decided to bite it back instead. She stormed off to her station behind her counter and began changing the cash register tape that still had almost ten feet left on it.

Knowing his comment was out of line, Roy was relieved that he wasn't lectured by Babs, particularly in front of the others. After only a few moments, he was back on his soapbox as if nothing had happened.

"What's needed are a few of those Molly Maguires to straighten out the mine bosses," said Roy, with his usual righteous attitude.

Harold shook his head in disagreement. "I don't think this town could deal with those thugs again," he said. "Although, I don't doubt for one minute that a few of them are still around, probably up in Jewett."

"What's in Jewett?" asked George.

"The Ancient Order of Hibernians," Harold hissed.

CHAPTER SIX

STROCK WASN'T SURE but he thought it might have been the sound of a whistling tea kettle that first shattered his sleep. Either that or it was the high-pitched squeak of the kitchen chair casters sliding against the linoleum floor. A new day had dawned .and the old lady was definitely up and about. *Hell, what time is it anyway?* he wondered. *Still looks dark, but at this time of the year, who can tell? For all I know, it could be seven o'clock. Why'd those bastards back at the jail take my watch anyway? Were they afraid that I'd build a bomb with it?*

Suddenly Strock heard voices and froze. His heart was beating so hard he thought it might burst through his chest. He listened, then relaxed some when he realized that the old lady had only turned on the radio, *The Breakfast Club.*

His stomach ached terribly and he wasn't sure if it was the liquor he drank the night before or the lack of real food. He couldn't remember the last time he had eaten anything besides homemade pies and icy milk and the whiskey the previous night sure didn't help any. He was now shivering so badly that at one point, he was sure he was about to screw himself right into the concrete floor. To ease the discomfort, he pulled his knees up to his chest and hugged his legs. He sat that way for several minutes, trying to block out the uneasiness, as well as the pressing need to relieve himself. His silhouetted body was gilded by the raging fire that burned in the furnace behind him.

Each day, he felt weaker than the day before. The icy beds Strock had slept in since his daring escape had drained him of his strength and one more night in the barren wilderness would have probably drained him of his will to go on. The air in the basement, though warm, was difficult to inhale because the old furnace sucked every bit of oxygen. His lungs felt dead.

If only he could get a cup of coffee and some toast. Unfortunately, he couldn't just barge through the cellar door and attack the old lady. She would probably keel over from a heart attack and die right on the spot. Assault with intent to ravish was one thing, murder was something all together different. No, he would wait until she left the house.

He sat down with his back against the boiler and watched as the rays of the new day's sun sneaked through the branches and cast their shadows against the far concrete wall. The faint images flitted like tiny dancers. *Am I going crazy?* he wondered.

CLINTON STROCK AWOKE with a start. Once again, he had fallen asleep. Although the concrete floor was hard — the paint-encrusted drop cloth he had found didn't cushion him much — the heat from the furnace acted like a sedative and kept knocking him out. He could barely keep his eyes open. *At some point, I've got to stand up and get the blood flowing,* he thought. *When's this old bag going to leave, anyway?*

The upstairs radio was still on and the smell of fresh coffee wafted down into the cellar. *What I'd wouldn't give for a hot cup of coffee and a shave,* he thought. His four-day old beard felt itchy.

When Strock thought he heard her footsteps moving into another part of the house, he reached over and carefully opened the squeaky furnace door. As far as he could tell, there was enough coal in the chamber to last perhaps one more day. Shit, w*here do I hide if she comes down here?* he wondered.

When he tried to stand, his legs felt weak and, at one point, he nearly toppled over. Finally, with the aid of the work bench, he stood and shuffled along the basement floor trying desperately not to make even the slightest sound.

Oh no, he groaned when he spotted a washing machine and wringer dryer along the far wall. *Please don't be laundry day.*

Using the light from the basement window, Strock found a full-sized pantry. He carefully opened the door but froze when it let out a terrible groan — the hinges were old and rusted. He proceeded cautiously. He peeked his head in and saw there was enough room for him to hide if she came down to do her laundry. If she happened to come for provisions, though, he was a dead duck.

Strock grabbed a 16-ounce can of Dinty Moore Beef Stew from the shelf and gingerly closed the pantry door. He located a rusty screwdriver lying atop the workbench, then returned to the side of the furnace where he had laid down the drop cloth covered with the dried paint. He sat and listened carefully. When all he could hear from above was the occasional creak of a floorboard, he got up on his knees, wiped the screwdriver on his pants' leg and slowly plunged it down through the steel cap. He did this several times until he was finally able to insert the shaft and pry up a small portion of the lid. He craned his head and listened again for the old lady. Still nothing. He poured the stew into his hand and ate like a ravenous dog. He did this repeatedly until the can was empty. He couldn't remember when canned food tasted so good.

Strock stood up and walked over to the opposite side of the basement and urinated into the used can of stew, careful not to cut himself on the jagged metal. Finally, he reached up and opened the cellar window and dumped out the contents. He hid the can under a cardboard box and returned to his station by the boiler. All he could do now was wait for the right moment.

FUNERAL SERVICES FOR both Mary Jo Stevens and Peter Koegel were performed by Reverend Duncan of St. Mark's Episcopal Church on Race Street. The Gothic Revival church with its Tiffany windows, gold marble, brass furnishings and English Minton tile floor served as a fitting tribute to two of Mauch Chunk's own.

"I am the resurrection and the life, sayeth the Lord: he that believeth in me, though he were dead, yet shall he live: and whosoever liveth and believeth in me, shall never die.

"I know that my redeemer liveth," the Reverend continued, "and that he shall stand at the latter day upon the earth: and though these bodies be destroyed, yet shall I see God: whom I shall see for myself, and mine eyes shall behold, and not as a stranger.

"We brought nothing into this world, and it is certain we can carry nothing out. The Lord gave, and the Lord hath taken away; blessed be the name of the Lord."

No funeral in the town had ever been so sad. It was the final good-bye to two children and no one in that church knew why God had chosen to take them so soon. While it was their province to bear God's burdens, not to question them, it was difficult for many to understand His mysterious ways nonetheless. The tears that flowed in the Church that morning attested to that.

THE CHIEF WAITED until nearly 3:00 p.m. before heading over to South Street to meet with Tom Stevens. Their house was up the hill from town, about an eight minute ride on 903 across the Lehigh River. This was going to be one of those awkward moments and he wasn't sure how he was going to handle it.

As he pulled up the block and nuzzled the vehicle next to curb, he noticed that all but one of the cars that had gathered earlier had left. The Dylan's white Chevrolet was in the driveway behind the Stevens' black Ford.

Chief Getz climbed the three front porch steps, rang the doorbell and waited. Ruth jumped slightly when she opened the door and spotted Chief Getz. "Oh hi, Lou. Sorry, you scared me. I didn't expect to see you up here. Come in, please," she muttered glumly while valiantly trying to smile. She had aged five years in the past five days. Her long jet black hair that once had luster now looked more like hay and revealed prominent streaks of gray. Her skin was chalky and her eyes were as lifeless as her daughter, who would have celebrated her 20th birthday the following week. A big piece of Ruth had also died.

The Chief removed his hat and said, "I'm terribly sorry for your loss, Ruth. If there's anything I can do, please don't hesitate .... " His words trailed off.

As tears welled up in her eyes, she again tried to smile with little success. Her lips trembled.

"Is Tom around? I'd like a word with him if it's not too much of an inconvenience."

Ruth nodded, then walked through the living room toward the kitchen. Chief Getz heard voices and assumed they were those of Duke and Kelly Dylan who were the Stevens' best friends.

As Tom Stevens appeared and shook hands with the Chief, Getz asked, "Tom is there some place where we can talk, alone?" Tom nodded and grabbed his winter coat from the hall closet. As they stepped out onto the porch, both men turned up their collars to buffer themselves against the cold October wind.

"What is it, Lou? What's so important that we have to talk out here?"

"Well, Tom, something's come up that you should be aware of. I didn't want to mention it to Ruth. I know how difficult it's been for her, for the both of you, ever since .... , well, you know."

Tom placed his hand on the Chief's arm, as if to encourage him to go on.

"I received a copy of the autopsy reports yesterday afternoon and, well, the coroner determined that both Mary Jo and Pete had sustained bruises on the back of their necks sometime that night, just prior to their deaths."

Tom cringed and Lou could see the agony on his face.

"Tom, the coroner thinks that they were both knocked unconscious prior to the hangings. He called it 'blunt force trauma'."

Tom Stevens was stunned. After a few moments, he sat down on the top step and rubbed his temples trying to make sense out of it all. "I don't think I'm following you, Lou," he said almost inaudibly. "Are you telling me that they didn't commit suicide, that they might have been *murdered*?"

"Yeah, Tom, it appears that we now have evidence that leads us to that conclusion."

Tom Stevens lowered his head and stared at the small bushes that lined the front walk. After a few moments, he raised his eyes and looked at the Chief. "Who, Lou? Who would want to murder my daughter, my beautiful daughter?"

"I don't know, Tom. That's why I need your help."

CHIEF GETZ RETURNED to the station around six-thirty that evening. Tom Stevens couldn't come up with anything helpful, nor could the parents of Pete Koegel who lived just two blocks over. They voiced what everyone else had already said, that both kids were happy and had never been in any kind of trouble. Mary Jo worked for a prominent tax attorney in town while Pete owned a small printing business over in Lehighton. They were God-fearing people who attended St. Mark's regularly. Neither smoked, drank, swore, gambled or consorted with known criminals. There were no jealous ex's, no unusual phone calls, mail or visitors. In fact, there was nothing out of the ordinary. Murder made as little sense as suicide and the 'whys' were just as difficult to answer. The Chief was drained, unable to come up with anything that made sense. His thoughts were scattered like the toys of a struck piñata.

To make matters worse, Annie had left a note on the Chief's desk earlier indicating that Ken Koslo wanted to see him first thing in the morning. In bold letters, Annie wrote that the Mayor sounded very upset.

STROCK WAITED MORE than an hour after the old lady went to bed before he dared get up and leave her basement. With the help of two wooden boxes, he crawled back out the tiny window and headed over toward the lake, a distance of one hundred yards.

When he was sure he was alone, he squatted down and relieved himself behind a large pine tree maybe twenty feet from the side of the lake. He used sheets of old newspaper that once lined the shelves in the basement cupboard.

When he reached the side of the lake, he sucked in the brisk night air, stretching his arms out as wide as they could go. How good it smelled and tasted, particularly after being cooped up in that cellar for so long. The air down there was devoid of oxygen and rendered the mind useless. Here, at least, he could think clearly.

Across the lake, the full moon rested precariously atop the peak of a steep hill like a huge orange ball balanced on a seal's nose. *If I wait long enough, maybe a stiff wind will blow it off and it'll come tumbling down and plunge right into the lake.* Strock smiled.

He removed his clothing and kneeled down by the water's edge. As the tiny waves lapped against his feet, he took a small handful of laundry powder that he had stuffed into his trouser pockets and bathed himself. His body odor had become so wretched that he couldn't even stand himself. While the water was frigid and he now smelled like Duz detergent, it was worth it, for Strock was again human, as well as several pounds lighter. As he allowed the cold breeze to dry him off, he squeezed his eyes shut, forcing himself to remain still. Then he quickly dressed and ran back toward the house, careful not to be spotted in the headlights of passing automobiles, ones that hurt his eyes before melting into blurs.

He quietly crossed over the side lawn, slid through the cellar window and grabbed another can of stew. Afterwards, he tried to think of a viable plan of escape but couldn't. The fresh air had taken its toll. He was too tired. He knew he would have to stay another day or so just to regain his strength, then it would be time to hightail it out of Mauch Chunk. Maybe he would move to one of those states out west, perhaps as far away as California. He pondered the various possibilities until his eyes closed and sleep covered him like a warm blanket.

CHAPTER SEVEN

"HEY, ROY, did you see it this morning?" George didn't wait for his answer. "The Dave Garroway Show, I mean. They were talking about our "Nickel-A-Week" drive, right there on the TV."

"Christ, George, you'd think they'd have better things to talk about than a stupid fund raising. Can't they program something worthwhile? To be honest with you, I'm not real sure this television thing is going to last. If you ask me, it'll never replace the radio. It's just a bunch of snow and static."

George interrupted. "Hell, if it was up to you, you'd outlaw the automobile, have everyone riding around in a horse and buggy just like those Quakers over in Lancaster County."

"Yeah, that probably wouldn't be a bad idea either. Wouldn't have all the congestion like we get nowadays."

"Yeah, and all we'd have to worry about is the horse shit piled along the curb."

"And what's so bad about that? We could use it to heat our homes. That way we could tell the mine owners to go to hell, tell them we don't need their goddamn coal."

Daisy shot Roy a look, an admonishment for him to hold his tongue. But Roy simply ignored her as he often did. What could she do? Not feed him? Hell, he was one of her best customers.

George was unrelenting. "While we're at it, why don't we do away with electricity, too. Candles work just fine and they're a whole lot cheaper."

"I never heard old Abe Lincoln complaining," said Roy.

"Jesus, Roy, just how old are you anyway?" He laughed.

Harold had finally heard enough and shouted, "Stop it! You're both driving me nuts."

Roy just shrugged his shoulders, wondering why Harold got so bent out of shape over these things. You see, Roy actually enjoyed arguing. In fact, the more stupid the argument, the better. He often thought it was too bad he couldn't earn a living at it since he felt it was his only remaining talent. So he opted to share his gift by irritating the hell out of everyone around him.

As the three men poked at some day-old coffee rolls, Billy Chalk entered the diner and sat at the counter, purposely down a ways from Roy's booth.

"Morning, Daisy. Man, I'll tell you, it's really bad out there, a real icy rain. Slippery as all get out. A person's got to watch their footing." Right on cue, the sleet clicked loudly against the diner's tin roof.

"What can I get for you this morning, Billy?" asked Daisy.

"The usual — two blacks, one with cream no sugar and one regular. Ring up one of those, too." Billy pointed to a cream-filled crueler in the glass display case.

"Hey, Billy, any luck finding that escapee?" Billy turned around and saw Roy, the exact person he was trying to avoid. He groaned.

Billy didn't much like Roy. He never did anything for anybody, but sure knew a whole lot about everybody else's business. Nevertheless, he gave Roy a courteous response.

"Naw, Roy, nothing yet. Some guy up at Summit Hill thought he spotted him yesterday, but the county boys came up empty."

"Seems to me that it's taking you guys an awful long time to find this guy," Roy continued, provoking a confrontation in the process. "Hell, between the Mauch Chunk Police, the County Sheriff's Department and the State Police, I'd have thought you would've nabbed him by now." Roy was now at his annoying best, *or* worst.

"It's not that easy, Roy. The guy could be almost anywhere. For all we know, he could be hiding out in your basement as we speak."

George Milosevich and Harold Seward both choked back laughter, while Daisy darn near spilled the cream she'd been pouring into one of the plastic cups.

"Well for your information, Officer Chalk, there ain't no way he could get into my basement. It's sealed tighter than a bulkhead." Roy was nearly spitting fire.

"I wouldn't be so sure, Roy. Might be a good idea for you to head home right now and check. God only knows what you'll find down there. I'd be real careful, though."

Harold added, "Yeah, Roy, maybe Billy's right, maybe you should go home and check it out."

As Roy's dander rose, he snapped, "Why don't you mind your own business, Harold. The escapee could just as well be down in your basement, you know."

"Hardly think that's possible, Roy," replied Harold, "since I don't have a basement."

Upon hearing that, George starting choking on his Pall Mall and, in no time, smoke billowed out of just about every orifice of his gaunt, crimson head. He removed his handkerchief and dabbed his eyes.

Billy got up and walked over to the booth. He knew he had caused a stir and that pleased him. A wry smile crept across his face.

"My point is, fellas, this Clinton Strock fella could be anywhere. If he's not hiding out in Roy's cellar, he could be in mine. But chances are, he's long gone by now."

Not willing to let it drop, Roy said, "Well I know he's not down in my basement. If I ever caught anyone down there, I'd blow his head clear off ...."

Billy cut in. "Now I wouldn't suggest you do that, Roy. That'd get you in a whole heap of trouble."

Roy turned his head and peered out the window. As he watched the hail bounce off the cobbled street, Billy returned to the counter.

"Don't be too hard on him, Billy," Daisy chided. "He's just a lonely old man who's got nothing better to do than to stick his nose into matters that don't concern him. He doesn't mean any harm."

Billy removed his hat and ran his fingers through his thick, dark hair. "Yes, ma'am, I know. It's just that of all the folks in town, Roy Gessler gets under my skin more than the rest." As usual, Billy tipped his hat, then started toward the door.

"Oh, Billy, one more thing before you go," Roy shouted, trying his damnedest to get in the last word. "I understand that the Mayor is a little more than upset with the police department. Seems that he's not too happy with the ways things are being run."

Billy smiled to himself, knowing exactly what Roy was up to. "Thanks for the tip, Roy. By the way, do yourself a favor, go home and check your basement." Billy then left the diner with the four Styrofoam cups of coffee and a smile on his lips.

Knowing that Roy was ready to explode, Harold and George merely chuckled under their breath.

WITHOUT WARNING, the header gave way and the walls began to crumble. This sudden cacophony of exploding rock and splintered wooden beams resonated in Strock's head. Blinded by the rush of surging coal dust that swarmed over him like a desert sirocco, he could feel the entire weight of the mountain toppling on him. The pressure on his chest was unbearable, laying like a huge stone. His heart raced as he gasped for oxygen. Finally, he coughed, then sucked in a huge mouthful of coal dust that billowed around his head. After all these years working for those bastards down in the coal mines, he was about to die a terrible death, the exact kind of death he had had nightmares about for the past twenty years.

Suddenly, Strock realized that he was not being crushed to death under tons of hard anthracite coal after all, but instead, had been awakened by the grating noise of a coal delivery at the old lady's house. The harsh raspy sound of the coal rushing down the hopper and crashing onto the coal bin had awakened Strock in a way he had never been stirred before. Even in the military, reveille was never as bad as what he had just experienced. It would take a while for his heart to regain its normal rhythm.

As a cold sweat ran down his face onto his collared shirt, Strock tried to brush off the mantle of coal dust. It was to no avail. The dust clung to him like moss to a tree. His scruffy beard was filthy and itched more than usual. Fearing discovery, he rushed over to the pantry, stepped inside and carefully closed the door. He waited and listened. He only heard two voices outside the house. *Probably the old lady and the delivery man*, he thought.

"YOU WANTED TO see me, Ken?" Lou peeked his head into the Mayor's office.

Ken Koslo had been the mayor of Mauch Chunk for sixteen years and by most accounts he had done a pretty good job. He was up for election next week — he was running against some guy named Hervey Breault who owned the Army-Navy store in town — and was odds on favorite to hold his seat for yet another two years.

Ken and his younger brother Earl owned Koslo's Feed and Hardware down on Broadway, had for twenty-odd years. Since Earl was the businessman in the family, Ken had time to do his politicking and was pretty good at it. With the local election just a few days away, he'd been doing more hand shaking than usual. He looked tired. The circles under his eyes were darker than the Chief remembered and the lines on his long face seemed deeper. The Chief figured he was at least partially to blame.

"Seems we have a problem, Lou. I got a call from Tom Stevens yesterday and he sounded pretty upset." Koslo paused for effect. As he drummed his fingers on his desk, he stared out his second-story window onto the busy street below. Rivulets of rain ran down the window panes like slimy worms. "Seems the coroner thinks that the two kids were murdered, that they didn't commit suicide after all. What do you know about this, Lou?"

"Yeah, I spoke to Harry Arnett on Wednesday. He found some bruises on the back of ...."

Koslo slammed both palms down on his desk. "I know all about it, Lou. Goddamnit, that's why I called you in here this morning. Why the hell wasn't I informed of his findings? You know this puts me in a very difficult position. I'm the mayor of this town and I don't know what the hell is going on. Why didn't you tell me when you first heard about it from the coroner?"

Getz started to respond but the Mayor cut him off. "I don't like being put in an untenable position when the entire town is panicking, Lou." His prominent wattle shook with each word he spat.

The Chief hesitated, trying to put his thoughts together. "Well, first of all, I wanted to make damn sure that he was right," he said as his stomach churned. "That's why I went up to the Stevens' house right after I spoke with Harry. I wanted to see if Tom could shed any light on this mess. I also sent Billy up there to look for any hard evidence that could corroborate Harry's conclusion. Billy also spoke with neighbors as well as some of Mary Jo's and Pete's friends."

"You should have let me know what you were doing, Lou." At this point, the Mayor was just inches away from the Chief's face. "I sounded like an ass when I spoke with Tom. Hell, I didn't even know that you'd received the autopsy reports."

"I'm sorry, Ken. It's just that I wanted to cover all the bases before I did anything. Harry's findings caught me off guard too."

"What did Billy come up with?"

"Not a thing. There were no fingerprints. Everything had been wiped clean before we arrived."

Calming himself, Koslo sat down behind his desk and began fingering his fountain pen. Finally, he looked up and said, "If it was murder, Lou, I want you to find the perpetrator, and fast. Damnit, Lou, things like this aren't supposed to happen around here. Do you at least have a suspect?"

"Right now, our only suspect is Clinton Strock, the guy who escaped from the jail last Saturday. The only problem is that he could be hundreds of miles from here as we speak."

The Mayor suddenly stood up and snapped, "So what you're telling me is that you've got no evidence, no leads and no suspect except some guy who might be in Oregon by now. Is that right?" The Chief nodded and the Mayor fell back into his chair. When the pressure was turned up, the Mayor often spun the valve so tight that the pot usually exploded.

Koslo was not one of Lou's favorite people and, although his duties as police chief rarely involved a heated confrontation with the Mayor, Lou still resented having to answer to him. The fact that Koslo had won the last election only because no one had bothered to challenge him didn't help, either. In spite of this, Lou tried to maintain his composure.

"What do you want me to say, Ken? We thought that the kids had committed suicide. Case closed. Then all of a sudden the coroner returns a verdict of murder. I don't know what to believe. We're doing all we can, Ken. We're just running out of options."

"Stay on it, goddamnit. Do what ever's necessary to come up with the assailant or assailants. This is a small town, Lou. We can't bury something as terrible as this forever." With the back of his hand, he brushed Lou away like he was an annoying gnat, a gesture that did not go unnoticed.

"By the way, Lou, did you put out an APB?" The Chief nodded.

"HEY, ROY, DID you hear that the Lehigh Valley Coal Company laid off another 175 miners over in Hazelton?" George said as he and Roy were polishing off their bacon, lettuce and tomato sandwiches and fries. The Governor is talking about setting up some sort or industrial commission to attract other industry to eastern Pennsylvania that'll provide jobs for these unemployed miners."

"Retrain them to do what? Needlepoint? Sell women's shoes? You can't retrain these people. Mining's in their system in more ways than those fucking politicians and mine bosses are willing to admit. You know as well as I do, they're hard men, hated by some for being members of a union, praised by others for having the guts to work down in the mines." For once in his life, Roy was making sense.

Disgusted, he pushed his plate aside, slamming it hard against the wall-unit juke box. Babs looked up but soon returned to what she was doing.

George stared at Roy in amazement. Roy paid no heed to his icy stare and continued to ramble.

"Shit, half of them have Black Lung and won't last more than ten or fifteen years anyway. So what's the use? It would be much simpler to simply take them all up to Summit Hill and shoot the lot of them, put them out of their misery. Cheaper too. These fucking politicians make me laugh."

Babs glowered at Roy and didn't much appreciate Roy using all that foul language in her establishment. She stepped around the counter and marched over to the booth occupied by the culprit and his trusty sidekick.

As she wiped her hands on her apron, she said, "Listen, you two, I won't tolerate that kind of language in here anymore. Especially from you, Roy. I don't know how many times I've warned you about your vulgar tongue. It's upsetting my other customers. If you don't stop it, I'm going to have to ask you to take your business elsewhere." Like a school teacher reprimanding two incorrigible students, she shook her finger at the both of them. "Do you understand me?"

George was the first to respond. "Sorry, Babs. I'll make sure he buttons his lip in the future."

On hearing that, Roy screamed, "Me? What about you? You're the one using the bad language." Roy knew he was lying through his teeth and reddened slightly.

Babs blurted out, "It doesn't matter which one is using the foul language. I just want it to stop. All right?"

Ashamed, both men nodded their heads.

When the ruckus finally died down, Harold Seward walked through the front door, then proceeded to shake the rain off his coat much like a dog would after an unwanted bath. Conscious of the fact that Roy hadn't waved him over like so many times before, he joined them anyway.

"What's up, guys? You both look like you've lost your best friend."

Roy responded, "Aw, it's nothing. Babs was just over here complaining about George's foul language."

"Me?" George hollered as his lips released a huge cloud of smoke. "What in tarnation are you talking about, Roy? She came over here because of what you said about the politicians." George moved his beady eyes back and forth to make sure no one was listening, then whispered, "I believe you referred to them as *fucking* politicians."

Finally, Harold interrupted the bickering. "Please, you two, just stop it." He heaved a heavy sigh. "I can't believe you two. Maybe that's what you two should dress up as tomorrow night, two ten-year-old brats."

George screwed up his face, then asked, "You mean for Halloween?"

"Yeah," Harold responded. "The fire department's giving away three hundred and forty dollars in prizes. Maybe you two could go as the Katzenjammer kids, maybe win yourselves seventy-five dollars for best costume."

Roy ignored Harold's comment. He hated Halloween. Every year, a bunch of snot-nosed kids threw eggs at his house.

"Any kid comes to my house will get a lot more than candy," Roy snapped. "I've got my air rifle oiled and ready to go."

"You're crazy, Roy," George said.

"Maybe yes, maybe no, but a man's got a right to protect himself and his property."

"Maybe if you acted more civil, Roy, they'd leave you alone."

"Damnit, it's too late for that." Roy spoke loud enough to bother the other patrons. "Harold, don't you have some place to go?"

The fact was, Harold did have somewhere to go, but since his presence in the diner was an irritation to Roy, he decided to stay. He could be just as obstinate as the man across the booth, just not as annoying. When it came to that, Roy was in a league of his own.

Ignoring Roy entirely, Harold grabbed George's arm and said, "I don't know if you're aware of it, George, but there's a group around here that's thinking about merging East Mauch Chunk and Mauch Chunk, then changing the name to Jim Thorpe."

Stunned, Roy stammered, "Jim . . ., Jim Thorpe, the Indian? What the hell for?"

Harold replied, "I guess to revitalize the area some. His widow's thinking about making a trip out here to look us over."

"They've got to be out of their cockamamie minds."

George looked over at Roy and knitted his eyebrows. "Jim Thorpe was probably the greatest athlete there's ever been. Maybe it wouldn't be such a bad idea."

Roy ignored George's comment. Instead, Roy snarled, "That's it, now I've heard everything." Daisy and several patrons craned their necks to see what had set this man off. "They're going to dig up some dead Indian and ship him here to Mauch Chunk."

"Shush, Roy, Daisy is watching us." George put his finger to his lips.

Roy was not about to be intimidated by Daisy, Babs or any other woman for that matter. "Why not over in Carlisle?" he barked. "Isn't that where he played football?

George looked at Roy and said, "Yeah, I guess. Roy, I think you've had your fill of coffee for the month. Why don't you head home, reload your BB gun and take some more nasty pills."

"I got a better idea, George. Why don't you light up another one of those fucking cancer sticks and cough yourself to death." Roy's invective was razor-sharp, wielded by a master swordsman. During all the hours they had spent together, Roy had never lashed out at George the way he just had. Disgusted, George got up from the table, put on his coat, then exited the diner cursing Roy under his breath.

Harold turned toward the window and watched George as he slowly walked up the street and disappeared around the corner. He looked so small in an overcoat once belonging to a larger, more spirited man. Harold then turned and glared at Roy before leaving himself. He, too, said nothing. He just glared at the man.

STROCK KNEW THAT he had to get out of the area, but was deathly afraid to make his escape for fear he would be caught and taken back to that God-forsaken dungeon they called the county jail. The old lady's cellar wasn't the best place in the world, but at least it was warm and there was plenty to eat. Granted, he was tiring of cold beef stew, but it was still better than prison chow or the frozen milk and berry pies he had eaten while on the lam.

The bathroom situation, however, was another story. Strock wasn't sure which was worse, the jail, where he was allowed two trips a day, or the old lady's house where he had to climb in and out of the tiny cellar window. All and all, considering every law enforcement group within a hundred mile radius was looking for him, he felt that it was better to stay holed up right where he was, at least for the time being.

Strock knew he had one serious problem, though. Sooner or later, the old lady would have to come down those stairs, either to do her laundry, get some food from the pantry or to shovel coal. He had to remain alert, a difficult task since the warmth from the furnace kept knocking him out. And what would happen if she came down and he was asleep? If she screamed, should he run over and subdue her, tie her up, threaten to kill her if she did anything stupid? *Man, how do I get myself into these situations?* he groaned.

He gazed up and saw snow accumulating in the brick window well. His decision had been made for him. As long as it was snowing, there was no way he was leaving his little nest. He would stay one more night, then hightail it out of Mauch Chunk, hop a train to the end of the line, no matter where it was. At that moment, he didn't care.

Suddenly, he heard the upstairs basement door open and he froze. Even with all his planning, he became confused, his mind running every which way. He sure as hell couldn't stay where he was, but without time to squeeze through the cellar window, running was not an option. And he couldn't very well hide in the pantry, for what if she was foraging for provisions and opened the pantry door? They would both have heart attacks. He stood motionless listening to his heart pound.

When her shoe hit the first step, Strock suddenly focused and quickly tip-toed over and hid beneath the cellar stairs. He squatted down behind some cardboard boxes and other accumulated junk, hoping that his presence would be lost among the shadows. Wiping the perspiration off his forehead with the back of his hand, he tried with all his might to stifle his heavy breathing. When she reached the bottom and walked over toward the furnace, he knew that she had not seen him for she passed without the slightest hint of suspicion. Either that or she was the bravest woman he had ever encountered. He swallowed hard, though, when she reached down for the shovel, then relaxed when she began feeding coal into the furnace. He squeezed his eyes closed and thought, *Sonofabitch, maybe I pulled it off.*

As he had discovered, his new vantage point concealed him no matter what her intent; whether she did laundry, retrieved food or shoveled coal. *This will be my permanent spot,* he thought. *Now I'll be far enough away from the furnace so I won't keep falling asleep.*

One other terrible thought quickly came to mind. Not only was the 'old lady' not that old but she was rather good looking. *Put it aside, asshole,* he thought. *I've got enough problems as it is.*

CHAPTER EIGHT

"MORNING, DAISY," GEORGE said as he greeted her on the front steps outside the Sunrise Diner. After fumbling with her keys, they finally entered. When she flipped on the overhead fluorescent lights, the lamps flickered, trying desperately to open their sleepy eyes.

"This has to be a first, you coming in the diner before Roy. God knows, I usually have to look at his sour puss first thing. Lucky me." She sighed but her smile stole some of the sting from her words. "Anyway, what can I get you, George?"

"Oh, just a cup of coffee for now, thanks."

Ten minutes later, Roy entered the diner, his hair matted from the melting snow. As he stripped off the heavy winter coat, he snorted, "Sonofabitch. Some bastard just side swiped me as I was coming down 903. The sonofabitch wasn't even looking where he was going." Roy had either forgotten all about his cutting remark to George the day before or had simply decided to sheathe his sword.

"Where'd he get you, Roy?" George inquired, also willing to forget the whole mess.

"On my back right fender. Sonofabitch. I'll sue the bastard for all he's worth. Goddamn filthy snow."

Roy was right in one respect. The snow that fell upon the coal mining regions of Pennsylvania was not the same snow that fell onto the higher elevations. Here it had to pass through the thick layer of coal dust that permeated the lower atmosphere. Even in the cold winter months, the air was always filled with black dust that filtered down from Summit Hill. Around the turn of the century, it was so bad that the workers could actually hear the clip-clop of the donkeys pulling the coal carts long before they could see them.

"Daisy, get me a cup of coffee." His tone was condescending.

Grabbing a cigarette from his pack with his narrow, dry lips, George asked, "Who hit you?"

"My good-for-nothing neighbor, Howard Savich, that's who."

As George blew out a billowing bluish-white cloud of smoke, Roy pressed on about how he planned to sue his next door neighbor. Hell, he would sue his own mother if he had to. At that point, George let out an agonizingly long sigh.

Without looking at Roy, George said, "So where's your car now? Did the police call a tow truck?"

Though it was none of George's business, Roy confessed that he had not called the police or his insurance company. His car was right across the street at the train depot.

George threw up his hands in disbelief. He hurriedly ground his Pall Mall into the ashtray and got up from the booth.

As he grabbed his coat off the hook and headed toward the front entrance, Roy shouted, "Hey, where the hell do you think you're going?"

Without answering, George flew out of the diner, almost knocking down Harold who was trying to enter at the very same moment.

"What's the matter with George? Is he sick?" Roy ignored Harold and watched as George tripped up the block.

When George returned a few minutes later, he said, "Christ, Roy, there's not a scratch on it."

"Oh, you're crazy. There's a huge gash on the right fender. You just didn't see it."

Exasperated, Harold threw up his hands to call for a time out, then begged for one of them to explain what was going on.

After George explained, Harold thought for a moment. "I know how to settle this, Roy. I'll go out and take a look at your car. Whatever decision I come back with will end this petty argument. Call it binding arbitration. Agreed?"

Both feuding parties reluctantly nodded their heads.

When Harold returned, he was shaking his head. "If only my car looked so good. There wasn't a mark on it, at least not as far as I could tell."

"For crissake, Harold, there's a .... "

Harold threw out a cautionary hand to stop Roy. "Binding arbitration. Remember?"

"The snow's probably covering it up," Roy said underneath his breath.

"Now hush, Roy," George barked. "We agreed that this would be the end of it. Besides the snow's let up some. I swear, you have to be the most argumentative man I've ever met. Can't you just let some things go by without throwing in your two cents?"

Daisy brought over a fresh pot of coffee and poured each man a hot cup. Oddly enough, it was her way of trying to cool things down a bit.

Harold tipped his head back and took in the aroma of the freshly brewed coffee that wafted up under his nostrils. He loved the smell of the Sunrise Diner, the unusual mixture of ground coffee, fried potatoes and bacon. He wasn't sure whether all diners were assembled with the smells already built in at the factory, or if they just acquired their delicious aroma over time. What he did know was that most good diners smelled exactly the same.

Roy took a swig of his coffee and, as if the previous conversation had never taken place, asked, "Anything more on that injun thing, Harold?"

"It's not an Indian thing," Harold barked. "His widow's just trying to find a proper burial ground for her husband. Why do you always have to be so ornery, Roy? God, you'd think they were trying to bury Hitler here instead of Jim Thorpe.

"A lot of folks around here feel that the if the plan goes through, it'll be a Godsend," he continued. "Maybe it'll stop the decline of progress in these parts, help our kids who will be around here long after we're gone."

Ignoring Harold's argument, Roy wiped the frost off the window with his shirt sleeve, then gazed out at the traffic that had backed up on the narrow lane that ran past the diner. Speaking over the sound of blaring horns, Roy shouted, "Hey, I don't give a jot or kittle about them. What about the town's current residents, people like you and me? What's it supposed do for us?"

Harold answered, "We can't always be thinking of our-selves, Roy. We've got to think about the future, about the kids who are growing up here now."

"Hogwash! I can't be thinking about them *or* the future. I have to concentrate on *now*. You and me, that's what's impor-tant. We don't have that much time left."

Since his kids had moved from the area years ago, it was not surprising that Roy felt as he did. If they didn't care about him, why should he care about them? Although sad, it provided some insight into why Roy had become so surly in his old age. Apparently, not everything was all his doing.

"Now, that's real forward thinking, Roy," said George in between coughs. "I've never met anyone who articulated a point so eloquently."

Just then, Randy walked into the diner, removed his aviator glasses and ordered three coffees to go.

"Appears you fellas are in for a busy night," snickered Roy. "Huh, Randy?"

"I suspect so, Roy. Halloween's always a crazy night for us. You of all people should know that." Randy smiled mock-ingly.

DESPITE THE EARLY snowfall, the Halloween parade went off without a hitch. It was hoped that participation in this year's parade would exceed last year's since many residents and local organizations joined in the six-division march. The town fathers were not disappointed. Prizes were awarded to the largest band, best float, best senior organized unit, most original costume, most beautiful, best appearing clown, most comical and the oldest, smallest and fattest paraders. Music blared, children laughed and neighbors, who hadn't seen each other all year, chatted non-stop. Almost everyone in town attended, even Margaret Wenzel, the lady who lived out by the lake. The only person who was conspicuously absent was Roy Gessler. He was home, sitting in a chair in one of his upstairs bedrooms. Cradled in his lap was a Daisy air rifle.

CLINTON STROCK FELT like some of the pressure was off, at least for the moment. The old lady had come down the stairs the day before to shovel coal and, later, did a week's laundry. It was a cat and mouse game. Each time she retreated up the stairs, he ran over and either dumped his shirt, socks and underwear into the washing machine, or retrieved the items from the soapy water. He dried the articles by laying them on top of the old cast-iron boiler. They dried in almost no time. Of course,.if the old lady had seen him huddled under the stairs naked as a jaybird, there would have been hell to pay.

It was already dark outside and the old lady had left the house about an hour earlier. Strock heard marching band music from faraway but couldn't figure out why or where it was coming from. He was about to find out, however. He had been cooped up in the basement way too long. He felt claustrophobic and a just a little bit nasty. He had eaten his umpteenth can of beef stew and it was now time to seek revenge on this tiny town that had locked him away like an animal in that tiny Cell 17 in the Carbon County Jail. *I swear, there were nights when I heard voices coming out of those old stone walls.* He opened the tiny cellar window and slithered out to secrete some venom on this God-forsaken town.

The sky was partially overcast and the heavy clouds that ambled lazily across it cut off most of the light cast from the half moon. Strock walked from the lake toward town, first through the woods by the road, then later along the lawns, hiding in the shrubbery, careful not to expose himself to a vigilant homeowner or a passing motorist. He dodged headlights and, when possible, tried to avoid the mercury vapor street lamps by crossing in the middle of the blocks.

Moving ahead, he turned toward the sound of the band music when suddenly something cold and damp fell heavily upon his head. His heart stopped and his blood turned to ice as the lifeless figure mantled him like a gigantic spider web, enwrapping his head in a sea of gauze. Instinctively, he thrust his arms upward, tossing whatever it was off his body. His heart beating like a jackhammer, he watched it sway back and forth in the cold night air, then realized that he had walked headfirst into a white bedsheet draped from a lower branch of an elm tree, not into a ghostly apparition as first thought. His labored breathing eased.

But he again panicked when he heard voices nearby. Shaking, he knelt, then ran over to a nearby bush. As he tried desperately to stifle the chugging of his overtaxed lungs, he sighed as he watched two children pass, no more than three feet away. One was dressed as a hobo, the other as Captain Video, and both carried orange and black sacks. *Of course, the ghost, the costumes, Halloween.* Strock laughed as he hit himself on the forehead with his palm. He knelt for a few minutes trying to gather himself.

After a few more trick-or-treaters ambled by, giddy from all the sugar they had eaten, Strock stood and craned his neck. Then, as though a miracle had just occurred, he spotted something. Across the street, on the porch under the outdoor light, sat a mannequin-like figure wearing a stuffed pair of trousers and a red flannel shirt. Next to it was a cut-out pumpkin with a burning candle inside. Would the shirt fit him? Who cared? Anything was better than the prison-issued khaki shirt that he currently wore. Besides, the temperature wasn't much more than thirty degrees and the snow continued to fall, although not quite as hard as earlier.

From the bushes directly in front of the house, he listened for voices. When he heard none, he tip-toed up the three porch steps and quickly snatched the dummy, then ran off to the side yard. He stripped off the shirt and put it on over his, wearing it like a jacket. It fit. Not perfectly, but good enough. He hugged himself around the middle. Now feeling a bit warmer, he left the yard and proceeded away from the sound of the music. It was now time for a little Halloween mayhem of his own.

CHAPTER NINE

IT WAS SOMETIME just before 11 p.m. The parade had ended and most of the townsfolk had returned to their homes, as had their kids who now lay sound asleep in their toasty beds, bits of hard candy still stuck to their tiny teeth. The streets were again quiet.

The flakes had stopped falling but a cold layer of snow remained, making skulking very difficult. The sound of his shoes breaking through the icy crust that had formed on the snow was amplified by the still night air. Seeing nothing at either end of the street, he tip-toed up the front porch and rang the doorbell. His lungs chugged like an out of control steam engine and his heart raced almost as fast. Nothing. He rang it again. After a few moments, an inside light came on as footsteps neared the front entryway. When the porch light flickered on, he heard the rustling of the bolt. *Come on, come on,* he groaned. *I don't have all night.*

Suddenly, as the door was pulled open, the intruder lowered his shoulder and burst through the heavy door, slamming headfirst into Ralph Ames, knocking him hard onto the pine floor. Ames was stunned and shook his head to clear the cobwebs. It didn't help.

When he regained his composure, he nervously stammered, "Who .... , who are you?"

The assailant, who appeared ten feet tall from his vantage point, straddled Ames and shouted menacingly, "Shut up! Get on your feet."

As he struggled to stand up, Ames repeated his earlier plea. "What's going on? Who are you? What are you doing here? You can't just barge into a person's home like this." The man ignored him.

Ames was pulled to his feet and pushed backwards toward the center of the house. When they reached the cellar door, the assailant ordered Ames to open it and head down the steps.

"Why? Why are we going down into the basement?"

"Just do as I say and you won't get hurt." He flicked on the light switch.

As Ames reluctantly backed down the stairs, he screamed, "You won't get away with this." Midway down, he tried to rush back up past his attacker, but a perfectly delivered blow to the base of Ames' neck rendered him unconscious. Ames slid down the stairs face first until his head hit the concrete floor with a sudden jolt. He was splayed like a gutted squirrel with his head laying at a peculiar angle on the bottom step. Blood oozed from his nose and mouth.

The assailant stepped over the body and, after he found what he needed hanging on the wall over the workbench — a piece of rope maybe eight feet long — he returned and grabbed Ames by his pajama shirt collar and dragged him off the stairs. He then sat on the bottom step and fashioned a knot. Adept at tying ropes, within minutes, the perfectly crafted noose was ready.

Ames, who lay face up on the cold concrete, was conscious but remained quiet. The only movement came from his fearful eyes that darted around the periphery of the ceiling. He squeezed them shut trying to rid himself of this nightmare.

The attacker moved from the steps and tied off one end of the rope onto the main sewer line and then threw the other end over water pipe. The noose dangled in the air and Ames watched as it slowly swayed back and forth. He knew what it was meant for.

Still immobilized from the blow to the neck, he slowly moved his head and looked up at this stranger who had suddenly disarranged Ames' ordered life. "Why? Why are you doing this?"

"Because of Cell Seventeen. You and your kind are the reason for the handprint in Cell Seventeen. You and the others must pay for the injustice."

With very little effort, the intruder dragged Ames across the floor with one arm, then slipped the noose around his neck with the other. Ames tried to scream but couldn't. Finally, he pulled the rope tightly over the beam, placed Ames on a metal chair, then stared directly into Ames' plaintive eyes. He smiled an evil smile and said, "Cell Seventeen." Then suddenly, he kicked the chair from underneath Ames. A chill raced through the already cool basement.

As Ames swayed back and forth, his lifeless eyes staring eerily at his executioner, the water pipe creaked a solemn and mournful dirge. He had died an ugly death without knowing why. Or did he?

After wiping down the areas he might have touched, the assailant replaced his handkerchief, retreated up the stairs and quickly fled, leaving the front door slightly ajar.

CHIEF GETZ GOT the call around 6:30 a.m. the next day. Mike Luedtke had discovered Ralph Ames' body when he had come by earlier. They were scheduled to go hunting that morning.

Exasperated, the Chief first called Randy at home. After explaining what had happened the previous night, he told Randy to run by headquarters and get the evidence kit, then meet him up at Ralph's place just as soon as he could.

The Chief hung up the phone only to snatch it up again to call Billy. After eight rings, Billy finally picked up the receiver and growled something unintelligible. The Chief outlined the situation as best he could.

As he ground the sleep from his eyes with his knuckles, he mumbled, "Suicide or murder, Chief?" Under the circumstances, it was an appropriate question.

Billy's thick brown hair was matted on one side as though he hadn't moved his head once during the night. He had worked the late shift and didn't relish the thought of going back on duty with only two hours of sleep.

"I don't know," the Chief responded. "Randy's picking up the evidence kit on his way over. I want to go over the place with a fine-tooth comb. We can't afford to miss anything this time. I'll meet you up there in a half an hour." He heard Billy groan just before replacing the receiver.

The Chief's last call was to Harry Arnett, the Carbon County Coroner.

One hour later, Chief Getz, Billy and two men from the County Sheriff's Department huddled in Ralph Ames' living room, a setting that seemed somewhat incongruous for a murder investigation. Because Ames was an avid sportsman, he had fashioned his home into a quasi-hunting lodge. Most everything was either wood or metal, including several rifles mounted on the walls. The only exceptions were the leather sofa and a huge elk head that hung from the wall over the hearth, one with wary eyes that seemed to follow the Chief wherever he went.

While Arnett was down in the cellar with the body and Randy was dusting for prints, two Sheriff's deputies were taking Mike Luedtke's statement in the kitchen.

The Chief was the first one to speak. "I don't want a contaminated crime scene so be careful where you step. And watch what you touch. Let me repeat, don't touch a *damn* thing."

The Chief turned and addressed Billy. "When Randy's done, I want you to check for trace evidence, hair, fibers, whatever. Don't overlook anything. Okay?" Billy nodded."

He then addressed the two men from the Sheriff's Department and told them to check outside, look for footprints, spit, broken twigs, anything, he didn't care what. If this was a murder, the assailant had to leave some sort of a trace. When they were done, they were to scour the neighborhood, check with all the neighbors, see if anybody saw or heard anything.

As both men left to complete their assignments, the Chief moved to the front door and spoke to some of the neighbors who had gathered on the front walk. He told them to return to their homes, that their standing around gawking was not helping the investigation, in fact, was obstructing official business. While they did move back, none of them actually left, opting instead to stand at the curb freezing to death in their bathrobes and slippers. As the Chief closed the door, he wondered what it was that attracted people to grisly crime scenes like this one. Morbid curiosity, probably, although if they had actually seen Ralph Ames hanging from that pipe, they'd never be inquisitive again.

He then walked back toward the kitchen. Since the front door had been left open most of the night, the house was bitterly cold. Actually, the Chief wasn't sure if maybe the chill wasn't from the grotesque cold that always accompanied death. He felt a shiver travel down his back. He turned up the thermostat in the hall, then heard a loud click through the floor boards as the furnace responded. *Maybe that'll warm things up around here,* he thought, clutching his arms with his hands.

The Chief stuck his head into the kitchen and asked, "Hey, Mike, you feeling any better?"

"Yeah, a little, I guess," Luedtke muttered. He looked like a man who had just discovered his best friend hanging in the basement. His face was the color of autumn snow, his hands were trembling and his eyes were almost as dead as the deceased. Like a photograph, the camera had robbed him of his soul, at least for this moment.

The Chief apologized, but stressed that he needed answers and Luedtke seemed to be the only one who had them.

"How'd you find him, Mike. I mean, why'd you bother to come into the house?"

His voice trembling, he explained that he and Ralph were going deer hunting. When he arrived sometime around 5:30, the front door was open, so he knocked. When he got no response, he entered. The next thing he noticed was that the temperature inside was freezing, but thought maybe it was because the door had been blown open by the wind. Maybe Ralph was in the shower and hadn't noticed. When he noticed that the cellar door was open and the downstairs light on, he stuck his head in the stairway and hollered down. Again, there was no response. That was when he really began to worry. He stood on the top step for a few moments trying to gather his courage before heading down to have a look. Finally, he descended the stairs. That's when he saw Ralph and ran back up to call the police.

Seeing tears well up in Mike's eyes, the Chief interrupted him. "You did the right thing, Mike. Let me ask you this. You didn't touch anything while you were down there?"

"I guess I held onto the banister when I went down. And I know I did the same when I ran back up the stairs."

"No, Mike, I mean did you touch the body?"

"No way, Lou. It was awful." He went on to explain that at first, he thought that Ralph was pulling some sort of Halloween prank, hanging in his pajamas from some sort of a body harness to make it look like he'd hanged himself. It didn't take him long, however, to realize that Ralph was dead.

He told the Chief that the first thing he noticed was a puddle on the floor, like Ralph had gone to the bathroom or something. Then he noticed that Ralph's feet and hands were all bloated and his eyes were staring right at him without really seeing him.

"It was awful, his face all blue like that." Luedtke looked at the Chief with pleading eyes, looking for words that would make everything all right again. "As soon as I realized that he was dead, I ran back up the stairs." Tears again welled in his eyes and, though embarrassed, he made no effort to wipe them away.

"Mike, I want you to think about this very carefully before you answer. You were Ralph's best friend. Was there any reason he'd want to kill himself?"

"Ralph would never commit suicide. He loved life and lived it to the fullest. No way, Chief. They'd have had to drag him out kicking and screaming."

Getz nodded his head in agreement, then looked over at the two deputies from the Sheriff's Department. "Are you through taking his statement, boys?" he asked.

"Yes, sir, we've got everything we need right here." One of the officers handed the Chief the three-page report. "What do you want us to do next, Chief Getz?"

"Wait here for a minute. Let me check with the coroner to see if he can give us an approximate time of death. I want you boys to check with the neighbors, see if anyone saw or heard anything around that time."

After the Chief found the cream in the Frigidaire, he poured two mugs of coffee, patted Luedtke on the shoulder, then descended down the cellar stairs. He carefully stepped over the coroner's medical bag and slowly walked over to Arnett. He tried to ignore Ralph Ames who lay at his feet covered by a painter's dropcloth, but couldn't. As he made a face, he handed one of the mugs to Arnett and said disgustedly, "This is God-awful, Harry. What the hell is going on?" Arnett lowered his head and said that he honestly didn't know.

To the Chief, the basement looked like most basements with a washer and electric dryer, a workbench, with all the necessary hand tools, and an old coal-converted oil furnace. The only difference was the body of a very dead Ralph Ames.

"Find anything?"

"Yeah, Lou, but you're not going to like it. Ralph seems to have the same contusion on the base of his neck as the other two."

"Damn!" The Chief removed his hat and ran his fingers through his hair. He looked forlorn. "Are you thinking what I'm thinking, Harry? Do we have a serial killer on the loose?"

Harry nodded, "Looks that way, Lou."

The Chief no longer had any doubts. Over the past seven days, three residents of Mauch Chunk have died by hanging and each one had sustained a hard blow to the back of the neck prior to death. To make matters worse, not one had any reason to take his own life. It left only one other possibility — murder.

"When do you think this one happened, Harry?"

"Well, without an autopsy, it's hard to say, but based upon his temperature, postmortem lividity and the stage of rigor mortis, I'd guess somewhere around midnight, maybe one o'clock. It was a while ago judging by the hardness of suffused blood." After removing his gloves, he wiped his face with his handkerchief.

The Chief let out a sigh, then asked Arnett what he thought the guy was using to deliver the blows to the neck.

"Hard to say. I suspect he didn't use anything sharp because there are no lacerations, no external bleeding of any kind." Arnett paused, then surprised himself when he blurted out, "I guess he could even be using the side of the hand, you know, like a karate chop."

"A karate chop?" The Chief was as astonished as the coroner. "Christ, Harry, wouldn't a person have to know what he's doing to be able to knock someone out with the side of his hand?" Both men jumped slightly when the furnace suddenly clicked off.

"Shit! gasped Arnett. "It keeps doing that. Scares the bejesus outta me."

The Chief sort of smiled to himself. Their reaction was indicative of the tension that had spread throughout this tiny town ever since the bodies of Mary Jo and Pete were discovered. When word got out about Ralph — and it would as long as there were folks around like Roy Gessler — it would be a wonder if anyone ever opened their door again.

Collecting himself, Arnett replied, "Yeah, he'd have to be trained, all right. Administered correctly, a heavy enough blow to the neck can kill a person. But it doesn't seem like he's trying to kill his victims, only incapacitate them. There's no question in my mind that the rope is the instrument of death, though, *not* the blows to the neck." Arnett hesitated and then asked, "Have your men found anything yet?"

"No, not yet. They're still working on it."

As two men from Harry's office put Ralph Ames into one of those ghastly black body bags and carried him upstairs and out to the van, Harry put a consoling hand on Lou's shoulder and they both climbed back up the cellar stairs.

After Randy finished dusting for fingerprints, Billy headed down to gather any trace evidence. In the meantime, the Chief and Arnett stood alone in the kitchen slurping coffee.

As the Chief hoisted his cup to his lips, he said, "What are we going to do, Harry? This guy could be anywhere."

"Well, let's hope this time he left something behind. He'll leave a signature sooner or later."

"I hope it's sooner, Harry. This town can't stand much more of this. They'll be after my hide if I can't solve this thing soon. The mayor's on my ass as it is."

As Randy entered the kitchen and asked what he should do next, the Chief told him to head over to the State Police lab right away, have them run whatever prints he had through central processing. Their records were larger and their equipment a whole lot faster.

As Randy departed, the two deputies from the Sheriff's Department re-entered the house in search of Chief Getz. Finding him with Arnett in the kitchen, one said, "Hey, Chief, we found some foot prints that seem to lead up to the house."

The Chief raised his eyebrows and thought for a moment. Finally, he said, "The problem is there were kids all over this area last night. There must be tracks all over the yard."

"Yeah, but these are size ten, maybe bigger. They're too big to be a kid's."

"All right, I'll tell Billy to make a plaster impression. Good work, boys. Maybe we have something, our first piece of solid evidence. Let's hope so, anyway." The Chief removed his hat and raked his hand through his hair. His smile masked all the doubts he still entertained.

CHAPTER TEN

MAUCH CHUNK TIMES-NEWS

ALLENTOWN, Sunday, Nov. 1st — An explosion on Center Street in Allentown Saturday night caused a massive fire that destroyed the commercial block between Fifth and Sixth Streets. Witnesses reported hearing the blast sometime between 11:45 and midnight.

The explosion destroyed the first floor offices of Pinkerton Investigative Services, the national detective agency, and the ensuing fire leveled six adjacent buildings including The Firestein Museum, one of eastern Pennsylvania's most highly regarded art galleries. Dooley Ryan, the night watchman at Pinkerton, was injured by the explosion and later died at Allentown Memorial. He had burns on eighty percent of his body, according to a hospital spokesman.

According to Byron Schmitt, Chief of the Allentown Fire Department, the cause of the blast is unknown and, although no person or group has claimed responsibility, foul play has not been ruled out. "Our boys will spend the next few days sifting through the rubble. If it was intentional, we'll know it."

The three-alarm fire was said to be under control at 3:20, Sunday morning. Other than Mr. Ryan, there were no other reported casualties.

"HEY, DAISY, DID you hear about Ralph Ames?" As Roy choked and coffee spilled onto his flannel shirt, he egested a muffled, "Shit."

Ignoring his last comment, Daisy said, "Yeah, Billy was in here earlier. It's a shame. I didn't know him *that* well, but he seemed like a pretty decent guy."

"No he wasn't," Roy countered. "He was one of the bosses up at the mine."

"For God's sake, Roy, so what? The man just died. Can't you show some respect just once in your life?" Daisy wiped her hands on her apron, an act that was perhaps more symbolic than anything.

"I *am* showing respect. If he was still alive, I'd tell you what I really think of him and the rest of those thieving sonofabitches up there." A vein nearly popped on his sallow forehead.

Daisy threw up her hands in disbelief. *How could one man be so rotten and uncaring?* she wondered. "By the way, how did you hear about it? The police just got back a few minutes ago."

"Oh, I hear everything. A few months back, I got me one of those citizen band radios. Anytime they use their two-way radios, I can listen in."

Daisy knew that Roy got off on being a busy-body but she never knew how much until now.

Just then, the diner door blew open as George breezed in.

As soon as he sat down, Roy said, "Hey, did you hear about Ralph Ames? As George flicked the snow off his winter jacket, he shook his head.

"They found him hanging in his basement, just like those two kids last week."

George caught his lower lip in his teeth. "Oh no."

Roy screwed up his face and said, "I didn't know that you knew him."

"Yeah, I knew him. He was one of the few guys up there you could talk to, part of a new breed that looked out for us miners."

"Well he didn't do anything for me," Roy snapped.

"What about the earplugs and the filter masks?"

"A lot of good they did. Hell, George, you've got the disease and you're coughing worse than ever. And I have trouble hearing out of this ear, all that heavy drilling equipment and all." Roy grabbed his right ear. "And what about the time the gust of methane sparked that underground explosion. Nineteen men were killed, for God's sake. Earplugs didn't do a lot for them. Did they? The mines have outdated technology, poor safety measures and shitty working conditions. There's no getting around that."

"Well, maybe not, but if there had been people like Ralph Ames around when we first started, I wouldn't be hacking the way I am now."

Although he never once brought it up, he could never understand why he had black lung and Roy didn't. Aside from Roy's time in the Army, they had both worked on Summit Hill. Still, George would not have traded places with Roy, not for one single moment. Roy suffered in his own way and it was probably more agonizing. It sure was just being around him.

As George lit up a Pall Mall, Daisy came over with a fresh pot of coffee fused to her right hand. "I don't believe you two. There was a hanging last night and you're more concerned about what the mine owners did or didn't do for you. For God's sake, show some respect for the man. He *is* dead, you know." She poured two coffees and stormed off.

"She's right, you know," remarked George.

"No she's not. Hey, I'm no hypocrite. If I don't like someone when he's alive, then I'm not going to grieve for him when he's dead." George turned his head, unable to hold his eyes on this man who only saw one side, the dark side.

Following Roy's interpretation of the Christian doctrine, free of all false additions and developments, Harold entered the diner and Roy whisked him over with another one of his patented waves.

"Hey, Harold, you hear about old Ralph Ames?" George could do nothing more than groan.

CLINTON STROCK DIDN'T have the foggiest idea what time it was when he awoke. As he tried to shake away the cobwebs that had somehow crept into his brain as he slept, the aroma of fresh-brewed coffee wafted under his nose. He would have died for a cup right about then, preferably with a shot of whiskey. Instead, Strock had to settle for another can of beef stew for breakfast. He swore if he ever got out of this mess, he would become a vegetarian. *Oh, what I'd do for a cigarette.*

When the old lady leaves, I'll run upstairs and use the facilities. Maybe I'll even heat up some of that coffee, he thought. In the meantime, he urinated in yet another empty Dinty Moore tin can, careful not to cut himself on the jagged metal top. He then quietly opened the cellar window and tossed the contents out onto the snow-covered lawn. He watched with some amusement as the warm liquid melted the icy snow. Catching himself, he groaned, *Damnit, Clinton, get a grip of yourself.*

Strock was exhausted. Because of his incarceration in the old jail — and now in the old lady's basement — he wasn't physically prepared for all that activity the previous evening.

Damnit, freedom is everyone's birthright and it shouldn't be denied for anyone, particularly not from a man like me. I'll pay these bastards back in spades. You can bet on it.

IT WAS SOMETIME after three when the Chief called Billy and Randy into his tiny office overlooking the Sunrise Diner. He informed them that he had received a call from the State Police who said that the only prints they could identify were Ralph's. All the other prints Randy lifted were either smudged or just partials, not enough ridge or loop delineation for a match.

The Chief removed his hat and scratched his head. "It's probably because of all the Halloween activity last night. There had to be two hundred kids out there and I'll bet you dollars to doughnuts that everyone of them had their sticky little paws all over that door knob." He replaced his hat.

Exhausted, he went on to say that just like the other murder scene, there were no prints on either the water pipe, the heater *or* the banister. He again removed his hat and placed it on top of his desk.

The Chief rubbed his face with the palms of both hands, then in a voice that had lost much of its fire, said, "Oh, by the way, the Sheriff's sending over that plaster impression of the footprint they found out in the side yard. It should be here within the hour."

"You know, Chief, that bruise that the coroner found on the back of Ralph's neck?" The Chief looked up at Billy and nodded.

"Well, is the coroner thinking what I'm thinking? That Ralph was knocked unconscious first, just like Mary Jo and Pete?"

The Chief nodded. "He won't be sure until he completes the autopsy. If it is another murder, then we know how they're being committed, just not who did it *or* why. Any thoughts?"

Billy responded first. He always did. He said that Danny Danzig, .one of Ralph's neighbors, was walking his dog sometime after midnight and thought he noticed a late-model blue car racing down Fourth Street. Although Danzig wasn't able to see who was behind the wheel, he did remember asking himself why would someone from outside the neighborhood be driving around at that time of night, especially at that speed.

The Chief sat up smartly. "Did he recognize the make of the automobile?"

"No, I pressed him on that but he wasn't sure, said they all look the same. All he said was that it was shiny, blue and, as far as he knew, didn't belong to any of his neighbors."

"Could he be more specific about the time?"

"Naw, he said he was half asleep and he wasn't wearing his watch. The dog's barking woke him up. Sometime after midnight, that's all he's sure about."

"That ties in with what Arnett said," the Chief remarked as he turned and gazed out the window. He crossed his arms, then rested his weary head on the palm of his right hand.

"Any thoughts, Randy?"

Randy squirmed in his chair like an unprepared schoolboy. After several moments of mental gymnastics, he finally formulated a response. "Well, they both happened on a Saturday night?" He phrased his answer in the form of a question.

"Yeah, that's right, Randy, and that might be significant. We'll just have to wait and see." Billy turned his head toward the window, raising his eyebrows disparagingly. He, too, was often amazed at what passed through Randy's lips. While the two officers managed to work side by side, Billy had little time for Randy's reckless ways. By the same token, Randy could not understand how Billy avoided military service, the obligation of every able-bodied man. Flat feet would never had kept him from becoming a soldier.

There was a knock on the door as one of the Sheriff's deputies entered with both the fingerprint report he had picked up from the State Police lab and the plaster impression neatly wrapped in cloth. He carried it as though it were a priceless da Vinci sculpture.

"Thanks, Deputy. Tell Tom I owe him one. By the way, how's he feeling?"

"You know, Chief, some days he's fine, others he just doesn't .... " The Deputy paused, managed a faint smile and made up an excuse to leave quickly.

The Chief carefully removed the shoe impression from the wrapping and held it up for the others to see. "Either of you ever seen a tread like this one?"

Billy took it from the Chief, then cradled it in his thick hands. You could almost see his mind at work. After several moments, he blurted out, "Chief, I know where this comes from. It comes from the jail."

The Chief, whose face was so screwed up it looked like a wrung-out dishcloth, asked, "What in tarnation are you talking about, Billy? What comes from the jail?"

"This shoe. I may be crazy but this sure as hell looks like the sole of one of those prison-issue shoes. You know, Chief, those heavy black shoes with the clunky rubber tread? If you want, I'll run it up to the jail and compare it to one of the theirs."

Billy wasn't positive, but he thought he remembered seeing soles like that during various interrogations over at the jail. Half of those wise guys put their feet up on the table just to remind the authorities who was boss. He remembered those soles because on several occasions, they were positioned but an inch from his face.

"If you're right, Billy, it means that Clinton Strock is right back on top of our suspect list. Go ahead, Billy, see what you can find."

Billy returned after nearly an hour. Normally, the trip to the jail was only a quick stroll up Broadway, but because of the snow that continued to fall upon the village of Mauch Chunk, the footing was treacherous and the run up there had turned into an odyssey.

He ran into the Chief's office shouting, "It's a match."

Billy explained that the warden had gone to the supply room, then showed him the shoes they issued to all long-term prisoners. He also checked their records and confirmed that Strock was issued a pair in March, a size ten and a half. The shoe and the plaster impression matched exactly.

The Chief threw up his hands and declared, "All right, fellas, now we're getting somewhere."

He stood and put his generous arms around the shoulders of his two officers. He told Billy to head back up and check with some of Ralph's other neighbors. "Press hard," he said, thinking maybe one of them would remember something from that night.

The Chief then turned his attention to Randy and, in a fatherly tone, told him to check with every car dealership within a twenty-five mile radius of Mauch Chunk to find out who had bought a recent-model blue 1953 automobile. He was to start with Hamm Chevrolet, Anthony's Kaiser and Petrole Plymouth, then work his way out. The Chief knew it was a longshot, but he had to pull out all the stops. He didn't want to be caught again with his pants down if Strock was able to prove his innocence.

The Chief also told Annie to get a hold of Motor Vehicle and obtain a list of all 1952 and 1953 blue cars registered in the area.

When the meeting broke up, the Chief put down the file he had been reading and put through a call to Tom Holmes of the Carbon County Sheriff's Department who in turn telephoned Lieutenant Arthur Champion at the State Police barracks over in Lehighton. Even though they weren't able to pick up any prints in the basement, Clinton Strock was now considered the main suspect in the deaths of Mary Jo Stevens, Peter Koegel and Ralph Ames. He was presumed to be in the area and was considered dangerous. A meeting of all three law en-

forcement agencies was scheduled for three o'clock that afternoon in Sheriff Holmes' office.

Chief Getz also called Mayor Koslo. To avoid another epi-
sode like the last time when he had failed to apprise the Mayor,
he scheduled a meeting to fill him in on what had happened
last night, the evidence they had found and the strategy they
were pursuing. The Mayor agreed to meet with Getz in a half
an hour. Because it was Sunday morning, the Mayor wasn't
particularly happy about leaving his family although he didn't
mind missing Mass just this once. Duty called and he was con-
fident that God would surely understand.

As the Chief got up to leave, Annie came into his office
and handed him a message that Margaret Wenzel had called.
"She said it was urgent, Lou."

"It'll have to wait. I'll call her when I get back from my
meeting." As he blocked his hat, the Chief strode off to meet
Mayor Koslo.

Before Randy left the station house, he made one quick
telephone call over to Wilkes-Barre.

CHAPTER ELEVEN

"HEY, DAISY, HOW about a bowl of your navy bean soup?"

"Oh great, Roy, that's all we need, your mouth and ass going off at the same time." Roy's sneer made George sorry he opened up his mouth.

Tapping her pencil on her order pad, Daisy asked, "Do either of you boys want the soup, too?"

"Yeah, I'll take a cup. Might as well fight fire with fire, if you know what I mean." George smiled wryly.

"What about you, Harold. Can I get you something?"

"Yeah, how about another booth."

Suddenly, Randy Furey blew threw the door, marched up to the counter and placed his hat on the hook above the NCR cash register.

"Shame about Ralph Ames," Daisy commented as she reached up for three Styrofoam cups from the top shelf. "Wonder why he did it?

"Oh, he didn't hang himself, ma'am. He was murdered. We think he was murdered just like them other two."

From the booth, a chorus of "Murdered?" rang out. "Who was murdered?"

"Ralph Ames," Randy replied, his look blank. "Well actually, Ralph Ames and them other two."

"Why do you think they were murdered?" Roy asked. "I thought they hung themselves."

"The coroner found bruises on their necks," Randy replied. "He thinks they were hit with something before they were strung up."

"Why?" George quickly asked, shaking his head. "Who'd want to murder Ralph Ames? And who in God's name would murder two nice kids like Mary Jo and Pete?"

"The Chief thinks it's that escapee, you know, the guy who busted out of jail a week ago." With that, Randy replaced his hat, grabbed his coffees and departed almost as quickly as he had entered. The news of the murders left the boys stunned.

"Can you believe it?" Harold lamented. "I wonder how Tom and Ruth took the news? I don't know which is worse, having your kid kill herself or finding out she was murdered. I do know that every door in town will be bolted shut tonight once word gets around about Ralph."

"Yeah," George concurred while trying to remember the last time he locked his door. "It's been more than seventy-five years since we had a murder. Now we have three of them in one week. I wonder why they always come in bunches around here?

"And the guy's still on the loose. What's this world coming to anyway?" The ash from George's Pall Mall fell and splashed into his coffee-spilled saucer.

Roy smiled sarcastically and asked, "I wonder what the widow Thorpe is going to think about our fine little town once she hears about *this* turn of events?"

"I don't think it'll make a difference," replied Harold. "From what I hear, she's committed to moving him out here."

Roy sighed, "I'd feel a whole lot safer if the State cops were on it rather than the Keystone Kops. I don't think Getz and the rest of them have the foggiest."

When a garbage truck came to a stop at the far end of the diner and the men began rattling the metal cans, the racket drowned out Harold's terse rejoinder. It was probably just as well since Roy didn't like his affirmations second-guessed.

WHEN THE CHIEF returned to headquarters from his meeting with the mayor, he called Margaret Wenzel. As it turned out, he wished he had called her when he first got the message. Margaret suspected that someone had been inside her house and maybe still was there. Although she wasn't absolutely sure, she thought some food was missing and sensed that something was wrong. And there was another problem. It had been more than a couple of days since she had stoked the furnace and, understandably, was afraid to go down into the basement for fear of who or what she might find. If she didn't replenish the coal soon, she would lose the heat and her pipes would burst.

The Chief told her to get out of the house right away, then quickly snatched up the phone, called Sheriff Holmes and told him what he had just learned.

"Margaret Wenzel?" questioned Sheriff Holmes. "Isn't she the old lady who thought she spotted Strock last week?"

"C'mon, Tom, she's not that old. She's a year younger than me, for God's sake." Getz chuckled. "Now I don't know if it's Clinton Strock or not, but I do know Margaret. I think we'd better check it out. Better safe than sorry. Will you call Champion over at the State Police barracks? I think we should probably meet here first so we can figure out some way to sneak out there without him spotting us."

The Chief slammed down the receiver, exited his office and told the dispatcher to get Billy and Randy on the two-way radio. After some static and a series of clicks, the Chief grabbed the earpiece and bent down over the microphone. When Billy was contacted, he was told to return to the station right away.

Randy was on Route 93 heading for Hamm Motors. The Chief ordered him to turn around and head directly over to the Wenzel house, take up a position on the east side of Broadway. It was a Code Yellow.

CLINTON STROCK HEARD the old lady talking softly on the telephone. *Why's she whispering? If she was talking to a friend, she wouldn't be whispering. She must be up to something.*

After all, he had been encamped in her basement for several days. Exactly how many days, he wasn't sure. He had eaten her food, used her washer and wringer dryer and, on several occasions, climbed in and out of that tiny cellar window. Maybe he wasn't as stealth as he once was and she heard him fumbling about down in the cellar. Maybe she just sensed another being in her midst. Then again, maybe one of her neighbors had seen him emptying out the Dinty Moore can earlier. He couldn't be sure.

In order to hear better, he quietly crawled up the cellar stairs, stopped midway, then listened carefully. When one of the steps creaked, he gasped. Had she heard him? No, she was still holding her conversation. He listened closely.

Oh shit, just as I thought, the old lady is talking with the cops. She knows I'm here. I've got to get my sorry ass out of here.

Strock scurried back down the stairs and scaled the boxes under the window. As he began to wiggle his body through the tiny cellar window, he suddenly spotted something shiny off at a distance. He rubbed his eyes with his knuckles. The midday sun had pushed away the dark clouds that hovered overhead for the past couple of days, its rays bouncing off a metallic object across the street. Strock brushed aside the snow that had accumulated on the window well, then stared out into the glistening light. He blinked his eyes again and again until an earthly form took shape. *Damnit! A police car.*

Strock slid back inside. He needed time to think. He couldn't make a run for it because he surely would be spotted. Besides, the mercury had plunged overnight and, even if he was lucky enough to elude the cops, he would probably freeze to death in the process.

He had no choice but to stay put. But if he remained in the cellar, they would trap him like an animal and take him back to the jail. The only other option was to take the old lady hostage. Why not? The cops wouldn't let anything happen to her. Strock could demand a car, a full tank of gas, some money and twelve hours lead time. He could be in Indiana in no time, maybe hide out in one of those abandoned coal mines south of Gary.

Strock sat on the bottom step for several moments with his eyes squeezed shut trying to psych himself. When he finally summoned the courage, he rushed up the stairs and burst through the basement door, shattering the side jamb and tearing off the strike plate. The racket was terrifying. Margaret Wenzel, who had just placed her hand on the front door knob to leave, turned her head abruptly, then froze. Her eyes bugged in terror. After nearly five days under the same roof, these two strangers had finally met face to face.

At the visage of this large, bearded man exploded into her kitchen with the ferocity of a howitzer, Margaret let out a terrifying shriek. At almost the same moment, the capillaries on Strock's face nearly erupted when he saw the color drain from her face, her stiff body slam against the door, then slide down into a lifeless heap onto the tile floor.

Oh shit, oh shit. What do I do now? I just killed her. The hair stood on the top of his head. He cautiously inched over, bent down and thanked God when he saw that she was still breathing. Uneven as it was, it was breathing, nonetheless.

Before doing anything else, he knew he had to go to the bathroom. With all the excitement, his bowels had been stirred. So with the police camped outside, his freedom hanging in the balance, he found himself seated in the bathroom staring at the sailboat wallpaper, then leafing through a copy of *Redbook* magazine. After that bit of urgency had been attended to, he returned to the kitchen and pulled out one of the chairs from the glass table, then sat down to plan his strategy. As he rested his head in his hands and gently began to massage his temples, trying desperately to stimulate his brain, he realized that nothing was coming to him. He rubbed his thickening beard but that didn't help either. Nothing. His mind was a total blank. Too much was going on and it was all happening too fast.

I know, I need some of that coffee. That'll clear the cobwebs. He located a mug on the drain board and poured out a cup of joe. *Hurry!* Although it was lukewarm, it still tasted like nectar of the gods. He tipped his head back, closed his eyes and smiled, savoring both the taste and the aroma. The smile slowly slid off his face. *I'm in a heap of trouble. There's no time for self-indulgence,* Strock chided himself.

IT WAS NEARLY noon when five vehicles carrying eight officers, nine rifles, two shotguns, a thousand rounds of ammunition, tear gas canisters and four bullhorns left the Mauch Chunk Police Department and slowly headed west on Broadway. Overkill? Maybe, but they didn't want to take any chances. Clinton Strock was most likely armed and they already knew he was extremely dangerous. Just look at what he did to those poor kids and Ralph Ames.

One by one, the vehicles lined up along the side of the road behind Randy's car. Randy smiled to himself. He felt important, like a leader, in charge. He felt a lot like he did back at Fort Bragg when he was a soldier, a commando, a somebody. Soon, reality took hold and the State Police were back in charge.

STROCK DIDN'T SEE the reinforcements. Only the front portion of Randy's vehicle was visible from his vantage point beside the front window in the woman's living room. It didn't matter. He knew he didn't have time to run past the rails and over the hill like he had a few days ago. No, this time he was trapped inside the place that had given him refuge for such a long time. Once again, he was hounded like a poor fox. This time, however, he had a foolproof plan.

The sudden shriek, "We know you're in there, Strock," shattered the cold air like an ice pick. "Come out with your hands up and you won't get hurt. I'll give you three minutes."

Lieutenant Champion's booming voice resonated through his brand new electronic bullhorn. All he had to do was pull the trigger and his voice was amplified ten-fold. Champion stared proudly at the new-fangled device, like a man who had just discovered the vaccine for polio.

The noise of the loud speaker startled Strock. It was not a normal sound. Aside from an occasional groan from Margaret Wenzel, the house had remained dead quiet. The only other sound Strock sensed was the thump, thump of his heart which at one point felt like it was about to explode right through his chest. He moved the drape back ever so slightly. *Shit, look at all the cops out there.*

The lieutenant checked his watch and waited. The contingent of nine police officers were strategically positioned along the perimeter of Margaret Wenzel's property. His deployment of the men under his leadership was perfect, textbook, in fact. There was absolutely no way that this guy Strock could escape without being apprehended or shot. Although the Lieutenant had never actually shot anyone before, he was prepared. After all, Strock was a wanted man, a killer, a menace to the State of Pennsylvania.

Back at the house, Strock ran to the kitchen and yanked back the kitchen curtain. *There's another one,* he groaned. He then ran up the stairs, two steps at a time, and entered one of the front bedrooms. As he stood with his back to the wall, he carefully peeled back the frilly curtain, so as not to be noticed, and peered out the window. *Shit! There's another one of those sonofabitches.* With perspiration running down his face, he left the bedroom, flew down the stairs and re-entered the living room. *What the hell should I do now?*

Lieutenant Champion checked his watch again. He looked at his men, then arrogantly declared, "Okay, boys, his time is up."

He picked up the bullhorn and repeated his earlier message, only this time, he said he meant it. Chief Getz winced when he heard Champion's codicil.

Knowing that the old lady was his only hope, Strock ran over to the front door and knelt down. He rubbed her face. Nothing. He gently slapped her. Still nothing. He sat down and cradled her in his lap and tried to talk her back to consciousness. "C'mon, lady, wake up. I know you're not dead. I can hear you breathing. You're my only hope. Wake up, goddamnit!" Margaret didn't budge.

"Strock, this is Lieutenant Champion of the Pennsylvania State Police." Champion's voice interrupted Stock's appeals to Margaret. "We have the place surrounded. Come out with your hands up. Surrender while you still have the chance."

Strock ran over toward the side window and peered out. He saw four of them out by the road. They were positioned behind their vehicles and two officers held rifles at the ready. He ran back to the living room. He grabbed a lamp, yanked the cord out of the wall socket and smashed the front window, breaking through the panes as well as the mullions. Shards of glass and splintered wood flew everywhere.

Strock then cupped his hands and shouted, "Listen, coppers. I've got the old lady in here. I'm holding her hostage so hold your fire unless you want to take her down, too." The distance between the parties prevented the officers from detecting the crack in Strock's voice.

The Chief groaned, "Goddamnit. What's Margaret doing in there?"

"I thought you said she had left the house," grumbled Lieutenant Champion. "This screws up everything."

"I thought she had. I told her to get the hell out of there."

Champion got back on the bullhorn. "Listen up, Strock. If you have her as you say, we need proof. We have to know she's okay." Changing his tone, he pleaded, "C'mon, Strock, you can do that for us. Can't you?"

Damnit! She's out cold. How in the hell did. . . . He suddenly lost his train of thought. Then, like a bolt, he raced over to the front vestibule, grabbed the woman under her arms and dragged her across the carpet, toward the broken window. He carefully brushed aside the larger pieces of glass with a nearby *Life* magazine. He knew that in order to pull this off, he had to make them think that she was conscious and unharmed. Maybe the distance between the two adversaries would work to his advantage. He grabbed her from behind, then pushed her up toward the open window, just so her face was showing a little. He took a large breath and shouted, "Okay, coppers, you satisfied?" With that, she slipped out of his grasp and fell heavily onto the floor with a crashing thud. *Shit!*

"We didn't see anything, Strock." The words resonated from the bullhorn. "You wouldn't be trying to pull a fast one, would you?"

Again, Strock pushed Margaret up with his left arm until her head was just over the window sill. With his free hand, he pushed open the drape just slightly. "Happy now, coppers?" he hollered.

Champion looked over at the Chief and laughed, "Who's this asshole think he is, James Cagney?" He suddenly turned serious again. "Hey, Lou, you know her. Talk to her. Ask her if she's all right."

The Chief complied. He grabbed the lieutenant's bullhorn and shouted, "Margaret, this is Chief Lou Getz. Are you okay?" The only sound that escaped from the speaker was a high-pitched squawk. Both men cringed.

"Just talk into it, Lou," chastised Champion. "No need to yell."

He repeated his message, only this time following Champion's instructions.

Strock hesitated. So many thoughts were rattling around in

his head, he cupped his hands over his ears to prevent them all from tumbling out onto the carpet.

Finally, a melodious response wafted out the window and across the lawn, barely making it out to the awaiting ears of the police. It sounded like, "Yes, I'm okay."

The Chief first looked at Champion, then commented, "She sounds funny, Art. I'm not sure it was her."

The lieutenant replied, "She's probably just scared, that's all."

Not aware that it was actually Strock's voice they heard, the Chief placed the bullhorn back up to his mouth and said, "Margaret, this is Chief Getz again. Don't do anything foolish. Do whatever he says. Everything will be okay. I promise."

Using his own voice again, Strock yelled out, "I don't want to hurt her, so listen up. These are my demands. I want $5000, a car, a full tank of gas and an hour lead time."

Now totally exasperated, Champion snatched the bullhorn from the Chief's hand and shouted, "You know I can't do that. Let the lady go. Don't make this any worse than it already is, Strock. Just let her go."

"No way! Now, either do what I say or I kill her." Margaret, who was now semi-conscience, heard Strock and squeezed her eyes closed as tightly as she could in an attempt to block out everything around her. She was about to die at the hands of some fugitive, a man who had already murdered three people.

The Chief looked at the State Police lieutenant and pleaded, "You can't let anything happen to her, Arthur."

"I know that, but I can't give in to his demands, either."

"For God's sake, Arthur, he's already killed three people. We don't need another dead body around here."

"He won't kill her, Lou. She's the only thing he's got. Without her, he's as good as dead." Lieutenant Champion opened the passenger side door and grabbed the two-way radio. "Let me check with headquarters."

The Chief walked over to the County Sheriff's car. When he saw Tom Holmes slumped over, his head resting on his arms that clutched the steering wheel, he became concerned and shouted, "Are you okay, Tom?"

Sheriff Holmes slowly rolled down the window and gasped, "I .... , I'm not sure, Lou. I don't f-feel too good. I feel like I'm gonna th-throw up." His voice was hollow and beads of perspiration cascaded down his ashen face. His breathing also seemed erratic. To the Chief, Tom Holmes looked like a man who was having a heart attack.

"Hold on, Tom." The Chief quickly motioned one of the Sheriff's deputies over with a sweep of his arm. "The Sheriff isn't feeling well. Take him to the hospital right away. We'll handle things here."

"Are you sure you .... "

"Just do it, Deputy," the Chief implored. "Hurry, there's no time to waste. Call dispatch and tell them what you're doing. Call me when you learn something."

The deputy took over the driver's side as the Chief helped Sheriff Holmes slide over to the passenger seat. The deputy did a K-turn, then sped off in the direction of the hospital. The rear of the vehicle fish-tailed on the slippery road.

Lieutenant Champion got off the two-way radio and stuck his head out the window. "What the hell was that all about, Lou?"

"I'm not sure, but I think Tom's having a heart attack. I told the deputy to take him to the hospital right away."

"Damn shame." With almost no hesitation, he continued, "Are we still covered on the rear flank?"

"Yeah, Billy's back there," the Chief replied. *How can Champion worry about that now?* he wondered. *Tom's having a heart attack, for God's sake.*

Champion exited the automobile, walked toward the rear and opened the trunk. As he hitched up his trousers like a Texas lawman, he looked down at enough weaponry to annihilate the city of Philadelphia.

"What are you going to do, Arthur?"

"I'll have one of my men fire tear gas into the house."

"Tear gas? The Chief's mouth dropped open in disbelief. Tear gas was used to flush out bank robbers and murderers, not to hurt people like Margaret Wenzel. Sensing the Chief's concern, the Lieutenant tried to calm his fears.

"Now, Lou, nobody's going to get hurt. We'll fire it in

through the side window. I'll move Teddy and Marvin up towards the front of the house. They can nab him when he runs out the front door."

"What happens if he comes out firing?" The Chief was visibly shaken. During his time as police chief, he had never faced anything this dangerous or scary. Guns, tear gas, a murderer? This was all unfamiliar territory and knowing that Champion was as green as he was didn't help any.

"Then we'll fire back." Champion looked at him quizzingly. "He *is* a murderer, Lou. Have you forgotten?"

"No, damnit, I haven't forgotten, but what if he uses Margaret as a shield? What are you gonna do, shoot her too?"

"Come on, Lou, I don't like this any more than you do, but I wasn't authorized to bargain with the guy." When Champion turned his back, the Chief grabbed his shoulder and spun him around.

"Listen, goddamnit. It'll be a whole lot safer for all of us if we just let him go. We can pick him up later."

Champion took his hand and removed it from his shoulder. "Can't do it, Lou. I have to follow procedures."

"This is what I think of your fucking procedures." The Chief flipped Champion the bird, then spent the next several moments wishing he hadn't.

Champion motioned for his two deputies to close in on the front of the house. A large rhododendron bush and a huge conifer tree were used for concealment. The lieutenant removed the rifle and grenade from the trunk and handed it to one of his officers.

"Son, take your position over there, by the side of the house. When I give you the signal, fire the canister into the house through the side window." He pointed to the exact spot. "Aim high and, son, be careful." As the deputy waited for additional instructions, Champion slapped him on the back and shouted, "Now, go!"

Champion took hold of the bullhorn. "This is your last chance, Strock. Come out with your hands up. Leave the woman in the house and exit through the front door. I've instructed my men to hold their fire. "You've got five minutes."

Champion walked back to the open trunk and replaced the

bullhorn. He had no further use for it. If Strock didn't surrender, he would resort to using more serious armament.

Strock sat with his back to the wall, his arms wrapped
tightly around his knees. He noticed the woman but paid her
no heed. She was no longer of any use to him. The hostage
ploy hadn't worked. Champion had either bluffed better than a
riverboat gambler or really didn't care what happened to the
woman. Strock suspected the former.

Margaret opened her eyes, closed them, then reopened
them. The light hurt. She tried to raise her head, but couldn't.
Instead, she panned the room until her probing eyes landed on
Strock. Fear again masked her face.

"Don't be scared, lady. It's almost over." He was resigned
to his fate.

"What . . ., what's almost over? Who are you?" Margaret
said, almost inaudibly.

"I'm the guy that everybody has nightmares about, the guy
who bursts into your life and disrupts your quiet, peaceful little
world. I'm the guy who keeps running to get away from
people like you, people who look down on my kind. But you
know what? The more I run away, the more I bump into
people just like you. I'm not sure whose nightmare it is anymore, yours or mine."

"What do you mean, people like me? I don't understand."
The pain was so intense that she barely whispered.

"You know who I'm talking about. The rich. People who
never busted their humps like me, who never went down into
the bowels of the earth for five dollars a day."

Margaret tried to laugh but could not. Instead she choked.
She cleared the phlegm from her throat and muttered, "I don't
know where you got that idea, but you've got it all wrong. My
late husband worked for nearly thirty years up at Summit Hill
before Black Lung got him. He fought in World War One, for
God's sake."

"Well I'm sorry about that lady, but I've got my own problems and they're right outside. The house is surrounded with
cops. They've given me five minutes to surrender."

"Are you the one who escaped from the Carbon County
jail?" He nodded.

"What about the three hangings?"

As Strock's mouth fell open, they both heard an explosion of glass from the adjacent room. As pieces of glass shot into the hallway, a strange hissing began and, within seconds, thick smoke lumbered into the living room like DDT. As soon as Strock saw it, he knew what it was. He had seen it once before during a prison riot.

As the miasma of heavy gas blanketed him like a fog-bound ship, Strock started to choke. His eyes burned and rubbing them only made it worse. He took out his handkerchief and slapped it against his nose and mouth. Nothing seemed to help.

Fortunately, Margaret remained prone and the cloud hovered just inches above her face. She coughed but not nearly as bad as her uninvited guest.

Strock had inhaled enough. Suddenly, he stood and felt his way to the front door. He unlocked the bolt and flew out of the house. His hands were held high just like they were supposed to be. As he collapsed in a heap on the front yard, he grabbed a handful of snow and rubbed it on his eyes. It relieved some of the burning.

Two deputies rushed over, guns at the ready, and stood over him like hunters standing over their fallen prey.

Strock coughed, "The old lady, she's inside on the floor in the living room."

Billy Chalk ran in through the door and, within seconds, led Margaret out the front door. Although she was choking, she appeared unharmed.

Champion bent down and looked Strock squarely in the eye. "Clinton Strock, you're under arrest for the murders of Mary Jo Stevens, Peter Koegel and Ralph Ames. Cuff him, Marvin."

Strock screamed, "What the hell are you talking about?" He coughed out the remnants of tear gas that were still in his lungs. "I didn't kill anybody." He resisted as the deputy tried to gather his arms behind his back.

Champion ignored Strock and continued, "The Chief here will escort you into town for arraignment before Judge Stone. After the charges have been read, you'll be returned to the Carbon County Jail. Do you understand me, Strock?"

"No, I don't understand a fucking thing. I didn't kill anybody. The only thing I did was to break out of that goddamn shithole you bastards call a jail. What's this about a murder?"

"Not a murder, Strock, murders. Three of them, in fact. No use trying to deny it. The evidence points directly at you."

Having just been accused of committing these heinous crimes, Strock dropped his head. He suddenly realized it was his nightmare.

Chief Getz went over to Margaret Wenzel and placed a consoling arm on her shoulder. "Are you okay, Margaret?"

"I don't know, Lou. It's been one hell of a day." She tried to smile but her eyes told a completely different story. She was frightened and the ordeal had taken a terrible toll.

"What happened? Did he hurt you?"

"No, I'm okay, Lou. Just a little shaken. I'll be fine." Lou realized immediately that she wasn't all right. She was shaking.

"I'll send Frank Jamison out to repair the windows and whatever else that might need fixing. It's probably pretty cold in there. He can stoke the fire for you. Maybe Marybeth can tag along, fix you something hot, make sure you're okay. I'll stop by later to see if you're okay?"

"That would be nice, Lou. Thank you."

"Randy will stay here until Frank arrives." The Chief told Randy to bag any evidence found in Margaret's basement. Randy nodded his understanding and proceeded off to his vehicle to retrieve the evidence kit from his trunk.

As the police vehicles wound their way through town, finally arriving at the Mauch Chunk courthouse, the Chief thought how angry Judge Stone was going to be once he was roused from his usual Sunday afternoon routine.

"I SAW A caravan of cop cars heading out Broadway earlier today and, by the looks of it, they're just returning now." George pointed out the diner window to the line of cars that inched slowly past the police station. "I wonder where they've been?"

"Probably a parade," Roy stated confidently. "They're always having parades around here. If it isn't the goddamn Italians, it's the Greeks or the Swedes." Babs came over to the booth carrying a full pot of freshly brewed coffee.

"You're awful crabby today, Roy," she chimed. "And from the sound of it, you must think they're all diseased or something. Who wants coffee?" When all three raised their hands, Babs poured.

"They probably *are* diseased," he snapped. "Most of them have scurvy, you know, from sailing over in those disease-ridden boats of theirs."

"You never cease to amaze me, Roy," George remarked as he shook out a fresh Pall Mall. "And what's this bullshit about sailing. They don't use sailing ships anymore. They fly in things called *airplanes.*"

Roy ignored George. Instead, he looked out at the frozen rain that had begun to fall. The headlights from the passing cars cut through it, making it look like bits of shattered glass.

Harold suddenly interrupted the silence. "Here comes Billy. Maybe he can fill us in."

After he had ordered three coffees, Billy looked back over his shoulder and commented, "Awfully late for you boys to be out. What's the occasion?"

"We thought you might be able to tell us, Billy. What's with all the activity this afternoon?" Roy feigned nonchalance.

"We just arrested Clinton Strock up at the Wenzel's place. Turns out, he'd been camping out in her basement all along."

Stunned, Harold asked, "Is she all right?"

"Shaken but she's fine. Frank and Marybeth Jamison are with her now." Billy removed his hat and ran his fingers through his short hair. Obviously still confused about something, he blurted out, "The problem is, Strock says he didn't commit the murders. Other than escaping from the jail a week ago, he says he's innocent of all the other charges." Billy knew right away that he had said too much.

"Of course he'd say that" Roy snapped. "Whaddaya expect him to say? That he's a goddamn killer?" Roy looked disgusted.

THE CHIEF SPENT a good part of Sunday evening interrogating Strock. They sat in that dank room on the third floor of the jail for almost three hours, just the two of them. No matter what tactics the Chief employed, Strock wouldn't budge. He said he didn't care what the charges were, he didn't kill anybody. *A guilty man's defense, if I ever heard one,* thought the Chief. Sometime around ten, Getz, now tired and frustrated, called the warden and Strock was escorted back to his cell.

As he exited the jailhouse, Getz wasn't sure who had suffered more, he or Strock. The temperature in that small, dingy room with the thick stone walls couldn't have been more than sixty degrees and the lighting continually flicked on and off, giving him a wicked headache. It had been a very long day and his face registered the day's extreme stress.

Not only was Clinton Strock back down in the bowels of that old jail, the catacombs that echoed the sounds of dripping water, clanking metal locks and heavy footsteps, but Cell 17 once again had his name on it. The guards — dressed in those ominous black uniforms — tossed him in and bolted the door. Any further trouble, they said, and he'd find himself down in the dungeon, a series of sixteen cells, some with marks of shackles.

So much for innocent until proven guilty, thought Strock. *And why did they put me back into Cell Seventeen? I can't sleep with that eerie handprint on the wall.*

The Chief didn't get the chance to stop by Margaret Wenzel's place like he'd promised. He did call, however, to let her know he was tied up with official business and would try to visit her first thing in the morning.

He looked forward to seeing Margaret and felt bad that he didn't have the time to go out to the lake to check on her well-being. He was sick and tired of this murder investigation and would have welcomed the diversion. He was worried about her.

The Chief drove straight home after the interrogation, threw another one of those TV dinners into the oven and watched the local news on the television. The lead story was the capture of the escaped prisoner Clinton Strock by the

Pennsylvania State Police. There was no mention of his department or the Sheriff's Department, for that matter. The Chief was too tired to care.

It wasn't long before he changed into his night clothes and plopped down onto his bed. This night, however, he wasn't thinking about his late wife but of Margaret Wenzel. He smiled.

THEY ARRIVED AT the Switchback Depot and took a seat in one of those pleasant summer cars that ran by gravity to the Mount Pisgah Plane. The plane was 2,322 feet in length, with an elevation of 664 feet, having a rise of about one foot in three. There were two tracks and upon each ran a safety car attached to two heavy iron bands that were six and one-half inches wide. These bands were fastened to iron drums, 28 feet in diameter, housed in the engine house.

The signal was given to the engineer at the head of the plane. The safety car was drawn slowly from the pit behind the car and the train began to ascend until it arrived at the top, nearly 900 feet above the starting point.

Lou placed his arm around his wife's shoulder as they braced for the release of the brake. They were poised over the mountains that overlooked the palate of colors God had readied for them on this glorious autumn midday. Bursts of sunlight exploded into yellow glitter and the air was as crisp as the emotions that raced inside their hearts. They had been so deeply in love ever since Helen's family moved from Hazelton during their sophomore year of high school.

Then suddenly, after passing through the engine house, the brake was released and the car lunged forward with a jolt. As the Switchback raced along the rickety track, they marveled as they sped toward the ravine that lay two miles below. From their vantage, they saw the Glen Onoko, the great falls, the crossing at Dula Vista, the Lehigh Valley Railroad Roundhouse, the Beaver Meadow Wharf, tier upon tier of mountains overlooking Lehigh Gap and the river that nosed its way through the Blue Ridge. At rapid speeds reaching fifty miles an hour, things whooshed by as frightened riders screamed for their lives. Their hearts pounded as they plummeted like a roller coaster. Finally, they reached their destination on the Mount Pisgah Plane where the train came to a complete stop.

Suddenly, everything looked different to Lou, as though he was seeing everything through white gauze. It was almost mystical. Before they exited the car, Lou leaned over, closed his eyes and kissed Helen. When he reopened them, he recoiled. It was not Helen he was kissing, it was Margaret.

Lou abruptly sat up in his bed, sweat pouring down his craggy face, his heart pounding just like it did during their harrowing ride down into the valley. After several moments, he realized that it was only a dream.

CHAPTER TWELVE

THE CHIEF WAS awakened at 5:32 a.m. by an impatient phone that seemed unusually shrill. As soon as he heard Annie's voice, he knew something was wrong. She said that Sheriff Holmes had died the night before, apparently of a heart attack. Getz groaned, mumbled something, then said he would get back to her.

He sat on the edge of his bed and ground the sleep out of his eyes with the backs of his hands. Or were they tears? A profound sadness stabbed him right through the heart, left him feeling as though a piece of him had also died. Lou had known Tom Holmes for nearly twenty years. When the Chief's wife was still alive, the four of them would get together, at least once a month. Both he and Tom were members of the same Masonic Lodge. In fact, Tom was a past Grand Master.

Lou knew that Tom's health was failing. Heck, just about everybody knew that. It wasn't just the way he looked, though. There were plenty of other signs. Most noticeably was the lack of fire in his belly. Somewhere along the way, he had lost his spirit. When the doctors first discovered the cancer, it was as if they had taken a piece of his heart and soul right then and there. And while he continued on as Sheriff and performed his duties responsibly, he just wasn't the same old Tom.

"HEY, HAROLD, OVER here." Roy beckoned him over with another one of his patented high-arcing waves.

Harold really wasn't in the mood for Roy's nonsense today. Nobody in Mauch Chunk was for that matter. Over the past few days, this small mining village nestled in the bosom of the Pocono Mountains had witnessed three murders and, although the person responsible was in custody, a pall lay over the town like a blanket of rotting leaves. No longer were doors left unlocked. No longer did folks run down into their cellars without, at least, some trepidation. No longer could Mauch Chunk enjoy the innocence that had made it what it was. No, these things were gone forever. Like so many other eastern towns, Mauch Chunk had been forced to grow up and enter the modern world that it had successfully avoided for so long. No one liked what they saw.

"Morning, Roy, George," Harold said. "Anything more on the prisoner?"

As Roy readied for yet another pontification, George pointed his nicotine-stained finger toward the door and said, "Here comes Randy. Why don't we get it from the horse's mouth." Roy looked deflated, like he had just been stuck with a pin.

"Morning, Babs," Randy said. "Three coffees and make 'em strong. I think today is going to be a long one." In an attempt to remove some of the ice, Randy whacked his heavy leather boot on the tile-covered footrest underneath the counter. The entire diner seemed to shake.

"How come, hon?" asked Babs as she poured the coffee into cardboard cups.

"Well, the Chief's going up to the jail to interrogate the prisoner and Billy and me are heading up to Ralph's place to try and find an eyewitness. It's going to be a late one for sure."

"Hey, Randy. C'mon over." Roy was his usual gracious self and barked the request more like an order.

After Randy paid and grabbed the paper bag brimming with coffees, he stopped by the booth. With a scowling face that spoke volumes, he said, "What is it now, Roy?"

"We were wondering if there's anything you can tell us about the Ralph Ames' murder. Did Strock confess yet?"

"Sorry, Roy, that's official business." Randy smiled contemptuously, then departed.

As George ground out his tenth cigarette in the metal ashtray, he said, "Man, oh man, I guess he told you, Roy."

"Told me what? He didn't tell me anything."

"Yeah he did. He told you to mind your own business."

"Bullshit. He said that it was official business and he couldn't give out any of the details. I believe him."

"Suit yourself, Roy." *Why do I even sit with this guy?* George thought to himself.

THE CHIEF COULDN'T bear the thought of spending another two or three hours questioning Clinton Strock. The news about Tom Holmes had sent a chill through his heart and he didn't need the gelid stone walls of the County Jail adding to his senses of coldness and despair. Since they had their man locked up tighter than a vestal virgin, the Chief decided to put it off for a couple of hours and take a ride up by the lake.

The snow that fell in the Poconos the previous night was a predatory one, heavy, wet and punishing. It fell awkwardly in huge, cumbersome flakes that attached to anything in their path. The snow that lay upon the bowed trees and overhead wires like wet canvas would later provide a day's rain once the sun mixed in its warmth.

The Chief drove past the police station and continued straight up Broadway out toward the lake. He had promised Margaret that he would stop by and see if she needed anything. But the truth was that he was going to see Margaret because, at that moment, he needed her more than she needed him. For the first time since he could remember, he needed to hear a woman's voice.

Aside from an occasional chirp of a finch or a sparrow, the only sounds he heard as he made his way up Margaret's front walk were his footsteps breaking through the ice and the wet snow falling from the crowns of the trees as they relinquished their burdens. Margaret greeted him at the front door.

"Good morning, Margaret. I'm sorry I couldn't make it by last night. Are you okay?" He wiped his boots on the door mat trying in vain to remove the stubborn snow.

"Oh, I'm fine, Lou." She told him that after she discovered her unwanted boarder, she felt violated, and felt a certain sickness in the pit of her stomach. That was why she was so appreciative that Marybeth had agreed to stay with her. She also mentioned that Frank had taken care of everything yesterday afternoon. He boarded up the two windows, made temporary repairs to the cellar door and said he would be back to replace everything else as soon as he could get his hands on the material.

Lou nodded. "I've got to ask you, Margaret, what made you call the station house in the first place? What made you suspicious?"

"The smell of beef stew," she laughed. "At first, I thought I noticed something odd when I went down to do the laundry — God, Lou, it makes me crazy to think that he was actually down there the whole time. Anyway, the odor just seemed to permeate through the entire house. I haven't had beef stew in months. I just knew something was wrong."

"Did you hear anything?"

"Not a peep." she shook her head. "Just smelled that damn beef stew."

"I wish I'd called you right away, Margaret. As it was, I had a meeting with the mayor. I should have called you first."

"Don't torture yourself, Lou. You had no way of knowing." She grabbed Lou's arm tenderly and asked, "What's the matter, Lou? You seem troubled."

"Tom Holmes died last night."

"Oh, Lou, I'm so sorry. Why don't we move into the kitchen. I'll pour you a hot cup of coffee."

Lou Getz and Margaret Wenzel spent the next few minutes talking about Tom, then moved on to their lives and how hard it had been on the both of them after the deaths of their spouses. It was odd. Although at first alone, for some strange reason bereavement overshadowed their loneliness. For the longest time, they muddled through, living each day at a time. As time went on, however, thoughts of their loss became less frequent, which was not to say they were over it. It just meant that their hearts didn't break every single day. It wasn't until they stopped grieving that loneliness reared its demonic self.

It was a quiet sort of ache, not a bullying, stabbing pain that comes with the initial shock of loss. Loneliness was suffocation. It sucked all the oxygen out of life. Loneliness was being trapped down in the coal mine with no air supply. All one could do was take short breaths until there was no more air to breathe. Tom's wife would go through these and other stages over the next few months, perhaps even years.

Only time had the power to heal, not well-meaning friends and family who tried so desperately to fill the void. But, as with so many things in life, Margaret and Lou had both learned to cope. And so would Tom's wife, in due time. It had been that way for Lou and Margaret for many, many years. Now, for some odd reason, they both pondered their aloneness and wondered why.

Lou really didn't want to give up the warmth he was feeling in his heart. He had enjoyed their conversation and couldn't remember the last time he had spoken so openly to anyone. As he was getting ready to leave, Margaret reached up on her tip-toes and kissed Chief Getz on the cheek. "Thanks for listening, Lou. Thanks for all you did."

The Chief somehow managed to start his car, do a K-turn and head back toward town without slamming into a tree. His mind raced and he was unable to grab onto any one thought. Something had just happened but he didn't know what it was. *No Margaret, thank you for being there for me.*

After he had made a quick detour to check out things back at the station house — nothing yet from Harry Arnett — he did what he had to do. He headed up to the Carbon County Jail to interrogate Clinton Strock.

"COME ON, STROCK, we have you dead to rights. Why don't you just confess and get this over and done with? We have all the evidence we need to convict you for the murders of Mary Jo Stevens, Peter Koegel and Ralph Ames."

"I don't give a shit how much evidence you think you have. I didn't kill anyone."

The Chief had been in that small interrogation room for less than 30 minutes and he was practically ready to confess himself. The mercury had plummeted overnight and the stone walls of the old jail did little to prevent the chill from penetrating the insides of the old jail. Both men continually wiped their noses and rubbed their hands together. With each breath, puffs of smoke exploded from their mouths, then ambled upwards only to disappear.

"The shoe impression is pretty weighty evidence, Strock. It's enough to get us a conviction."

"You're wasting your time, Chief." Strock puffed his cheeks without taking his eyes off of Getz. "If you're here to force a confession out of me, you're wasting your time. You're going to have to look for some other sucker to help you." Strock picked a piece of lint off of his trousers.

"Okay, Strock. Let's go over this one more time. Where were you on Saturday night, around midnight?"

"Like I said, I was holed up in the old lady's basement. I heard some music and decided to go see what all the fuss was about. I'm not denying that I was out that night. I *am* denying that I had anything to do with those murders."

"Well, how'd your footprint wind up on Ralph Ames' property?"

"Hell, my footprints are probably all over town. I was on a lot of people's lawns. I even stole a shirt off of one of them dummies sitting on a front porch. It doesn't mean I killed anybody."

"Did you know Ralph Ames?"

"No, like I told you before, I never met the man. Hey, I'm no Boy Scout, but I'd never kill a man. Hey, you've got to believe me."

The Chief spent another full hour with Strock with the same results. In an effort to loosen him up, the Chief even had the guard get Strock a real cup of coffee and a pack of Lucky's. While Strock relaxed a bit, he still vehemently denied any wrongdoing other than parking his ass down in Margaret's basement without her knowledge and, later, stealing a flannel shirt off a front porch. The Chief was at his wit's end. While he hadn't expected Strock to confess right off, he had hoped to find a hole in his story. But each time he recounted the activities of Saturday night, he told the same old thing.

The Chief's other problem was motive. Why would Clinton Strock kill three residents of Mauch Chunk, three people he'd never met? Revenge against his captors?

THE CHIEF ARRIVED back at the station around eleven-thirty. He was drained. The murder investigation was wearing on him and Tom Holmes' death had hit him hard. *Hell, I'm supposed to be tough and impassive,* he groaned. His main thought at that moment was of leaving town, removing himself from the madness that had exhausted him both physically and emotionally.

Just as soon as the glass door sealed behind him and his foot hit the shiny white and black tile floor of the Sunrise Diner, the Chief knew that he should have spent the extra money and had lunch at the Hotel Switzerland. Instead, the first thing he heard was his name being bandied about by none other than Roy Gessler. Just like earlier up at the jail, a cold chill went up the Chief's spine and turned right around and traveled back down. He wasn't particularly fond of Roy under normal circumstances and sure as hell didn't need his bullshit now.

"Hey, boys. Howya doing?" The Chief tipped his hat and smiled sardonically.

"How's it going with the prisoner?" Roy said. "Has he cracked yet?"

"Not yet, Roy. We're working on it, though." The Chief's tone was condescending. "I'll be sure to let you know when he does, Roy." The Chief winked at George who smiled.

"Maybe, if you want, I can help you out." Roy was dead serious.

The Chief laughed out loud. "Roy, the only way you'll be of help to me is to keep your nose out of my business. I know that'll be tough for you, but I assure you, I don't need you or anyone else doing my job."

The Chief walked over to the counter and ordered a coffee — cream, no sugar. He had lost his appetite and decided to return to police headquarters instead. He felt bad about snapping at Roy, but knew that even during normal times, Roy was a huge pain in the butt. Heaven knew, these were not normal times.

"I wonder what got his shorts in a bind?" Roy wondered out loud after the Chief departed.

"Probably you and your big mouth," remarked George.

"Why don't you give the man a break. He's doing the best job he can."

"What did I do? I was just trying to help out."

"By offering your services? What the hell do you have to offer?" said George.

"Hey, you guys seem to have forgotten that I was a member of the Third Army, part of the Allied Army of Occupation. One of my jobs was to interrogate the Krauts after the occupation. I was pretty good at it, too. Those poor bastards were scared as hell, afraid we were going to gun them down right there in the streets, just like back in the wild west days. They called us 'krazy GI's'. Actually, it was *verruckt*."

"I thought you were an infantryman in Italy," said George.

After a slight hesitation, Roy responded, "Ah, ... I was, but that was before they transferred me up north."

"Good grief, Roy, you're so full of crap you make a shit hole look like a powder room."

As the hairs on the back of George's neck tingled, he turned toward the steamy window, rubbed it with his hand, then watched as the pedestrians meandered along the street. Most were returning to their jobs, something he wished he still had.

WHEN THE CHIEF got back to the station, there was a message on his desk that Harry Arnett had called.

"A real shame about Tom. The county lost a good lawman," Getz groaned.

"Yeah," Arnett said, "it's really terrible. I feel bad for Dora. She's been through so much over the past few years. First Tom's cancer, then their son dying over in Saipan, and now this." His voice quivered slightly.

"Any word yet on the funeral arrangements?"

"I haven't heard anything yet, Lou. I'll let you know as soon as I hear something." Arnett hesitated, then continued, "This may seem like an inappropriate time to bring it up, but they've asked me to be acting Sheriff, at least until the county can find a suitable replacement."

"You're kidding?" The Chief chuckled, then caught himself. "I'm sorry, Harry, it's just that I never thought of you as a lawman. I thought you were taking the County Treasurer's job?"

"Oh, that won't start until some time in January. Hopefully they'll find a full-time Sheriff by then. Maybe they'll ask you, Lou."

"No thanks," The Chief groaned. "There's enough crap going on around here. I don't need the extra aggravation. By the way, Harry, before you put on that ten-gallon hat and strap on your holster, do you have the results of Ralph Ames' autopsy yet?"

"Yeah, Lou, I just finished my report. But you're not going to like what I found."

He said that based upon the state of rigor in the small muscles, lividity and the suffusion of blood, he placed Ralph's death somewhere between midnight and one a.m. Ralph's body temperature back at the lab was 88.1 degrees, which confirmed the time of death. He explained that under normal temperature conditions, the body cools between one and two degrees an hour. The temperature in his basement that night was seventy-three and well within normal limits. Unlike a body found out in the cold, the temperature in the cellar probably had no influence on the frigidity of the corpse.

The Chief placed his feet up on the desk and asked, "Hey, Harry, what did you mean before? You said that I wasn't going to like your findings."

"Well, yeah, this report is a virtual carbon copy of the autopsies I did last week on the two kids. Just as with them, I didn't find any hair or fibers under his fingernails so most likely there wasn't a struggle. In fact, there was no trace evidence anywhere. And just like with the other two, Ames had the same sort of bruise on the base of his neck. At some point that evening, he'd been knocked unconscious. Did you guys find anything?"

Scratching his head, the Chief replied, "Naw, everything down in the basement had been wiped clean."

"That's too bad. I guess it was a stroke of luck you found that shoe print, though. Has the guy cracked yet?"

"No, and he's not showing any signs that he will." The Chief said remorsefully. He had hoped that other evidence would tie Strock to the crime as well. An open and shut case is what he needed.

"Keep in touch, Harry." As the Chief was about to put the phone down, he snatched it back up and shouted, "Hey, Harry? County Sheriff, huh?"

Arnett laughed, then hung up the phone.

"WHERE'D HAROLD SAY he was heading?" Roy liked to keep his finger on everyone because, in his mind, if he didn't, his world would explode into flames and disintegrate like an ash from one of George's Pall Mall's.

"He said something about going up to the Dimmick Library. He had to dig into some old files or something," George replied. "He said he'd be up there the rest of the afternoon."

"That's odd." Then, changing topics as fast as he changed his moods, Roy blurted out, "Hey, Babs, what's it take to get another cup of coffee around here?"

Babs looked up from counting the morning's receipts and said, "Civility, Roy. That's all. Just a little civility."

As Babs poured, Roy asked her if she had heard anything about the funeral arrangements for Ralph Ames.

She replied, "Yeah, tomorrow at ten, up in East Mauch Chunk, at the First Reformed Church."

Scrunching up his face, George asked, "Why do you care where the service is, Roy? You haven't changed your mind. Have you?" George blew a huge puff of smoke over Roy's head.

"No, I haven't changed my mind. You'd just think that the guy would be a little more considerate, that's all."

"What in tarnation are you talking about?"

"I'm saying that him having the service way up in East Mauch Chunk is inconsiderate."

George dropped his head and banged it repeatedly on the table.

STROCK PULLED HIS legs up and lay them heavily on the foot of the narrow bed. The dampness from the cold, damp floor of Cell 17 had somehow transuded the rubber soles of his shoes and up into his legs. His joints felt soggy as though he had spent hours wading through the muddy deposits out by the lake.

He covered himself with the coarse horsehair blanket, laced his fingers behind his head and stared up at the ceiling. It was all he could do. Staring at the handprint on the opposite wall was driving him insane so he avoided looking at it.

The large black spider, the same one that had been his cell mate ever since he was first arrested, was still there. Like mingled yarn, it spent all of it's time spinning an intricate web up near where the ceiling met the windowed wall. Spinnerets under it's abdomen produced the silk used to make the web. It was a slow, arduous process, but the spider would not be denied. All day long, it wove. Strock wasn't sure what the spider did at night, for the lack of illumination deprived him of this one diversion to an otherwise dreary existence in that cell.

Pickings were slim but every so often an unsuspecting bug would fly into the spider's lair and become the day's choice morsel. Strock spent most of the lighted hours watching the spider. The problem was there just wasn't anything else to do. Jail in Mauch Chunk meant isolation, strict discipline and minimal living conditions. All that was missing were the beatings and floggings that prisoners endured back in the 1870's, back when the mystery of Cell 17 first began.

Most of the time, it was too dark to watch the spider so Strock would try to ignore the scratching noises the rats made and wait for the next sliver of sunlight to pierce through the narrow window up near the ceiling.

Then, each night before falling off to sleep, Strock removed his belt and quietly rubbed the shiny buckle against the concrete wall behind his cot. Any residue was carefully swept up and flicked out the tiny opening in the cell door. Each night, the edge of the buckle was honed a little sharper.

Like death, Strock was sentenced to eternal darkness, in a

crypt with a three-foot thick archway that mantled a solid iron outer door, as well as an inner door with bars spaced so close together that an open hand couldn't fit between them.

His days had been just as claustrophobic down in the coal mines. There was so little light in his day that sometimes he thought his other senses had become heightened, which wasn't always a blessing. Prison chow wasn't something a man wanted to savor, and listening to the plodding footsteps of the screws, the rattling of the keys and the clanking of the heavy metal doors resonated in his head, sending chills down his spine. There was little or no conversation aside from the half hour a day out in the yard. Even then, who would Strock talk with? He wasn't one of them. Strock was a decent man who had merely fallen on hard times. He wasn't a hardened criminal like the others. *So why am I in here and why am I now being accused of murder?*

Clinton Stock's past had been yanked from him so hard and so fast that he really didn't know who he was any more. His life had disintegrated from something into nothing. The relatively happy child had become an unhappy thief and batterer now confined in a cold and damp cell at the Carbon County Jail.

Strock leaned over and placed his head into his palms. He began to cry. *They're never going to believe me. They know that ever since I got fired from the mine a few months ago, I've skirted the law. Who's going to believe a jailbird who's known for his lying?*

His sobbing became so loud that a prisoner across the corridor screamed for him to shut up. Strock couldn't remember the last time he cried. *Maybe when Daddy died*, he thought.

He heard the heavy footsteps as they marched down the corridor and stopped abruptly outside of his cell. The guard looked in through the small barred window, inserted the key and opened the door.

"Somebody here to see you, Strock." The voice sounded like an echo.

Strock swung his legs off the bed, stood up and accompanied the guard down the corridor and up the narrow metal stairway. The guard made sure that Strock was in front at all times.

When they reached the interrogation room on the main level of the prison, the guard said to Chief Getz, "He's all yours. Whistle when you're through."

"You might as well get comfortable, Strock," the Chief said. "We're going to be here for a while."

The Chief interviewed the prisoner for the better part of two hours. Like the time before and the time before that, he was unable to illicit anything incriminating. Strock admitted being out that night and even conceded that he was on Ralph Ames' property. He admitted just about everything except to killing Ralph Ames. As far as the two kids, yeah sure, he was on the lam that night, but no where near town. He was out by the railroad tracks waiting to hop the next freight train out of Mauch Chunk. It was at that point that Strock learned from the Chief that the rails were from the old Switchback gravity railroad, a nine-mile run up to the mine. Even if it had been operational, Strock wouldn't have gotten very far.

A dejected Lou Getz left the jail and headed back to the station house. Again, Strock had stood his ground and, once again, the Chief had to admit that he really didn't have much to go on. Yes, Strock was out both nights, but there was one huge hole in the Chief's case: motive. Why would a virtual stranger to the town of Mauch Chunk kill three of its citizens? Aside from the one battery charge, Strock's personal and criminal history revealed little more than bad judgment and a nasty temper. The Chief even surreptitiously checked the sides of Strock's hands for any bruises. There were none, and Strock appeared confused when asked about any involvement in the martial arts.

To top everything else off, Strock volunteered to take a lie detector. The Chief knew that a polygraph wasn't admissible evidence in a court of law, but just for his own satisfaction, he was tempted to go out and find somebody that could administer the damn test. He was sure that somebody over at the State Police barracks in Lehighton was trained in that procedure.

The Chief mused that it was perhaps time to pack it in as Chief of Police of Mauch Chunk. Considering the recent crime spree, maybe he just wasn't up to it. In the past, his real police work consisted of little more than a stolen item here, a fist fight there and routine matters like traffic accidents and minor disputes. Never before had he investigated a murder, much less three of them. He was afraid that he had lost his focus. He knew that he'd already made some critical mistakes.

He had agreed to run the department six years ago at the urging of the current mayor. Getz had retired from the Mauch Chunk Police Department after nearly twenty years and taken a job over at Duquesne Industries, a manufacturer of industrial belts. After a few years as foreman, he retired and was just beginning to enjoy his simple, carefree life. Fishing eight or nine months a year wasn't all that bad. Then his wife died and his life fell to pieces. After several months in virtual seclusion, it finally dawned on him that he needed a distraction. At the time, though, he wasn't sure he wanted the job as Chief, or even if he was qualified to handle it.

Now, that same man who had once coaxed him out of retirement was squeezing the Chief for results. One of the messages lying on his desk was from Mayor Koslo who wanted him to call as soon as he got in. Annie underlined the word *urgent* twice. He ignored the message. At that moment, he couldn't deal with pressure from a man who himself was under immense pressure from the Mauch Chunk citizenry. After all, the election was but days away. He also ignored a message from Mauch Chunk Times-News' reporter Chick Devaney. Getz had nothing new to tell him.

Around four that afternoon, he convened a meeting with Randy and Billy and, for the first time, admitted that he had serious reservations about Strock's involvement in the recent rash of killings. Strock just didn't fit the profile of a killer, much less a serial killer. Accordingly, he told Randy to resume his check with every car dealership within a twenty-five mile radius, compile a list of anyone who had bought a brand new blue automobile within the past six months. Likewise, Billy was to return to Ralph Ames' neighborhood, check again for eye witnesses, anyone who might have seen anything. In particular, he was to press Danny Danzig on what he saw that night. Randy was to obtain photographs of all makes of cars for Danzig to look at. The Chief would check with The Department of Motor Vehicles.

"WE DIDN'T THINK you'd be back, Harold. Whatcha been doing up there at the library?"

"Geez, Roy, how'd you know where I was?"

"George here told me." Roy watched with glee as George melted onto the plastic seat cover like ice on a hot skillet.

"So what's going on," Roy pressed. "What's so important that you had to spend all them hours up there looking through those fancy books and all?"

"I was going through a few things that don't concern you any." Harold was put out. "I *can* go to the library without reporting in with you two. Can't I?"

"Why all the secrecy, Harold?" Roy furrowed his brows. "Damn, you make it sound like we're asking you for the formula for the atom bomb."

"Like if I tell you, you're not going to blab it all over town." Harold snickered.

"Suit yourself, Harold, it's no skin off my nose. I don't really give one hoot one way or the other. You could be looking through old National Geographic magazines for all I care." Roy threw up his hands in exasperation.

There was one good reason why Harold wanted to keep his research quiet, at least for now. He had a hunch. Something tied these brutal killings together and it was much more than some poor soul like Strock out on a crime spree. Because all the victims had died by hanging, Harold sensed that the goings-on over the past few days were somehow linked to the town's grim past. But what was the common thread? He had made some headway, but it was much too early to present his findings to the Chief. He certainly wasn't about to tell these two blowhards across the table. Like any good newspaperman, Harold was determined to research all his leads first, compile the relevant data and then and only then, write his prize-winning story.

Harold downed his cup of coffee, then announced that he had to go.

"Be here tomorrow?" Roy asked matter-of-factly.

"Maybe later in the morning. I've got some things to do

first." Harold was purposely being as evasive as possible, one to annoy his adversary across the table and, two, because it was none of Roy's concern.

"You know, Harold? You're a cipher wrapped in an enigma."

Stunned, Harold said, "Where the hell did you hear that expression, Roy? That doesn't sound like you at all."

"I heard it on The Video Theater last night."

"I thought you said that you didn't watch TV." Harold seemed genuinely surprised.

"I don't," Roy said smugly. "I was listening to it."

Harold looked over toward George for some help. When he got none, he ordered a cup of coffee to go, watched Daisy as she deposited it into a brown paper bag, then departed through the front door of the diner.

BEFORE CALLING IT a day, Lou Getz returned Mayor Koslo's earlier call. The Chief could sense the ice water flowing through the telephone line. Koslo wanted to meet with the Chief first thing the following morning, have him lay out everything he had, from the evidence gathered, suspects, hunches, the works. The murder investigation wasn't moving fast enough, according to the Mayor, and he wanted the Chief to jump start it. The storekeepers were nervous, fearful that the string of hangings would effect retail sales in Mauch Chunk. Annie was right. The Mayor was definitely pissed.

Those bastards, thought the Chief, reflecting on the store owners. *They don't care about the three victims. All they care about is the almighty dollar.*

When the Chief got home, he flipped on *I Led Three Lives* and promptly fell asleep in his easy chair. It had been a strenuous day and the next day promised to be more of the same. The folks around town had begun calling the station house asking if Strock had confessed yet. *Hell, how do I answer them?* he wondered.

An hour or so later, the Chief awoke and ambled to the kitchen, scratching his behind in unison with his shuffling feet.

Scratching his behind was part of his thinking process. He never could figure out why that was, it just was.

He opened the Frigidaire and stared into it for the longest time, as though he was awaiting divine intervention from one of the food gods. When he realized that he would get none, he squatted down and removed two plates wrapped in tin foil. He placed two lamb chops in the broiler and cut up some green beans and put them in a pot of salted water on the top burner. He didn't mind cooking so much, it was the eating alone that bothered him most. Ever since his wife died, he dreaded the idea of sitting in front of the tube, alone. Actually, he sort of liked those TV dinners he had purchased over at the A&P and wished he had one right then instead of the chops. Along with a glass of beer and a piece of buttered bread, he nestled into his chair in front of his two-year-old Zenith television and ate off his metal lap tray.

During the second half of the Eddie Fisher Show, Getz finally screwed up his courage and called Margaret Wenzel. No, she wasn't doing anything special and, yes, she appreciated his thoughtfulness. Sometime during their conversation, he became acutely aware of the framed photograph of his late wife that sat on the telephone table, the one that stared lovingly up at him as he spoke with Margaret. Without thinking, he took the picture in his left hand and placed it face down. He and Margaret spoke for another twenty minutes before he cradled the receiver and headed off to the bedroom. Once in bed, he stared up toward the ceiling for what seemed like hours before he flipped off the blanket, retreated to the living room and stood the photograph back up on its support. He returned to bed but had difficulty falling off to sleep.

CHAPTER THIRTEEN

"LOU, YOU'VE GOT to understand my position as mayor of this town. The folks around here are very nervous and they have every right to be. I'm getting calls all day long asking me what I'm doing to solve these crimes. What am I supposed to tell them, Lou? That we're working on it?" His voice rose. "Believe you me, that kind of response isn't going to cut it around here, not for long, anyway. Lou, these are simple folks. They don't understand how things like this can happen. All they know is that they want some action and they want it *now*."

Koslo got up, walked around to the front of his mahogany desk and stood toe-to-toe with the Chief. "The people around here won't be able to sleep until they know for sure that the man up at the jail is the murderer.

"Hell, I've got to attend another service today because of that crazy sonofabitch. And another thing. I hear the widow Thorpe is getting a little nervous about moving her husband's body over here. Do you know what that would do to this town, Lou? It would be devastating. We need closure, Lou. I want you to crack this case, get a signed confession from this Strock guy today."

When Lou started to object, Koslo held up his hand and said, "No buts about it." The Mayor drove his index finger into the Chief's chest for emphasis. When the Chief brushed his hand away, they stood eyeball to eyeball for several long, uncomfortable moments. The heaviness was finally broken when the Mayor wisely stepped back and returned to his chair behind the desk. It was a good thing because the Chief was a hair away from laying Koslo out across the top of it.

He had never seen the Mayor so exorcised but thought it might have something to do with the upcoming election. Despite Lou's assurances that he and his department were doing everything possible, the Mayor persisted. The Chief even went so far as to hint that he thought they might have the wrong man, but it didn't dissuade Koslo one bit. He was intransigent. In his mind, they had their man and no one was going to convince him otherwise.

"Lou, this has to end. The people around here have to know that it was a stranger, not one of their own. They have to unlock their doors, start going about their business, just like before. We have to put this all behind us, put the town back the way it was."

That was how the Chief's day began and as it progressed, it didn't get much better. When he arrived up at the Carbon County Jail for another session with the prisoner, he ran into Jeb Tully who was entering at the same moment. Tully, an attorney who ran a two-bit operation from his tiny office up on Race Street, had agreed to represent Clinton Strock.

Tully was a weak, sniveling man more known for chasing ambulances than for defending hardened criminals and the Chief did *not* need any more obstacles impeding his criminal investigation. Unfortunately, that was exactly what Tully turned out to be, another rut on what had already become a bumpy road. A little man with a little mind, Tully had a unique way of getting under a man's skin, much like a tick, then sucking out the lifeblood of his prey while fattening himself up in the process.

With counsel by his side, Strock became even more arrogant. At one point, Strock said that if the Chief continued with his line of questioning, he would clam up in protest. At least five times, Tully warned the Chief about badgering his client. Each time, the Chief told the ambulance chaser to shut the hell up. In the end, though, the Chief got nothing, not even conversation. As before, Strock declared his innocence.

"Justice shall prevail," Tully shouted.

Frustrated, the Chief shot the so-called attorney a look and departed.

Following Ralph Ames' funeral up at The First Reformed Church, the Chief received further confirmation that his day was not going to get any better. Danny Danzig was unable to ID any of the pictures in the dealerships' brochures of the different makes of new cars. Danzig told Randy they all looked the same. Besides, he admitted that he was half asleep at the time and really wasn't paying much attention. All he knew was that the automobile that sped away that night was metallic blue and looked fairly new.

Following the Chief's orders, Randy compiled a list of three people who had purchased a blue car within the past six months. That was the good news. The bad news was that the Chief knew every one of the new car owners and could vouch for each one of them. Randy was to continue after lunch and keep at it for another couple of days.

"The Department of Motor Vehicles is as useless as tits on a bull," said the Chief. He told the others that the Commissioner down in Harrisburg advised him that the department had recently installed some sort of newfangled punch-card automating machine that was supposed to do the work of hundreds of people. He said there were only one hundred of these so-called computers in the world. The long and the short of it was that until they get the bugs out or tore the damn thing out, he wouldn't be able to capture the information the Chief needed.

"I don't know why they picked us, Chief Getz," the Commissioner had groaned. "I was happy with our old system. I thought it worked pretty well." Getz could sense the man's frustration pulsing right through the phone line.

"I GOT IT!" Harold shouted, as other researchers near him looked up with dismay. Harold didn't care because, at last, he knew what it all meant. Well, most of it, anyway.

While ex-newspaperman Harold Seward had initially spent time up in the genealogy section of the Dimmick Memorial Library, he had moved his research over to Harrisburg, to the Hall of Records, where he dug through volumes of public records at the Pennsylvania archives. He started with only a name and, genealogically, worked his way back in time. Finally, after painstakingly plodding through what seemed like hundreds of names, he unearthed what he was looking for, the common denominator that might help the Chief solve this crime. His memory, one honed on years of investigative reporting, had served him well. He still didn't know the 'who' yet, but he may have found out the 'why'.

GEORGE ENTERED THE diner and shivered noticeably as he hung his heavy winter coat up on the rack over the booth. His teeth still chattering, he said, "From the looks of it, Roy, we're in for a long, hard winter. It feels like it's going to snow again."

"Tell me about it. The scary thing is winter doesn't officially start for another month and a half. Maybe I should move to a warmer climate, maybe Florida. While we're up here trudging through wet snow, freezing our you-know-whats off, they're down there lounging by the pool, sipping piña coladas."

"You'll never leave this area, Roy. You've lived here all your life. Mauch Chunk is too much a part of you."

"Don't be too sure about that, George. As soon as they change the name of this town to Jim Thorpe, I'm out of here. The fact that they're even considering it chaps my butt."

Aware that they were traveling down that same long road to nowhere, George changed the subject. "I see you're a man of your word, Roy. You didn't bother to attend Ralph Ames' service this morning."

"Like I told you, I .... "

"I know, I know," George interrupted. "We've already been through all the reasons. You don't have to rehash them." George removed his Pall Malls from his shirt pocket and slammed the top of the pack repeatedly on the Formica table.

Roy hesitated for a moment, then unleashed his abusive tongue. "That's very annoying, you know." George stopped, looked up at Roy, then twisted off the cellophane seal. A cloud of silence hung over the booth for almost a minute.

"Not that I give a hoot, but how was the turnout?" Roy finally asked.

"At the church, you mean? It was packed. Just about everybody in town was there. It was a nice tribute to the man. God knows he deserved it."

Roy lowered his head, then simply grunted, "Hrrumph."

As George ignited yet another cigarette, Daisy meandered over with a pot of coffee and poured two cups. "With all the coffee you two drink, it's a wonder either of you can sleep a wink."

Roy said, "It doesn't bother George none because he pisses it all out in five minutes anyway." He threw his head back and laughed as though he had said something terribly amusing.

"I've told you more than once about your language, Roy. You've got to watch it. The other customers don't like it and complain." Roy feigned concern, then giggled as Daisy walked away. He then asked George if he had heard anything more about the murders.

"I heard that Ken Koslo is at his wits' end, worried sick about losing the election. Apparently, he blames Lou Getz for everything. From what I hear, if something doesn't develop soon, he's going to take some drastic action. Do you have any idea what that means?"

Roy simply shrugged his shoulders.

IT WAS ALMOST five when the Chief got the call. The Mayor was hot and became even more enraged when he was told that the prisoner had not yet confessed.

"Lou, I want you in my office in ten minutes and I don't want any of your lame excuses."

The Chief knew something was up. He had never heard the Mayor so upset. Not wanting to incite him any more than he already had, he grabbed his hat and left his office immediately.

As the Chief sat in front of the Mayor's desk, the Mayor got up and began pacing back and forth directly behind where Lou was seated. This unnerved the Chief to no end. If the Mayor was about to unload something, he wanted it told to his face, like a man.

"Lou, the reason I asked you here is so you can hear it first hand from me." He hesitated for a moment to gather himself, then continued. "I'm sorry to have to say this, Lou, but until further notice, you are hereby relieved of your duties as Police Chief of Mauch Chunk."

The Chief's jaw dropped and he sat for the longest moment, speechless. Finally, when it sank in, he yelled, "You can't do that, Ken." The Chief's words were strained and unconvincing.

"Oh, yes I can, Lou. I'm in charge of this town and its well-being is my primary goal. We have a murderer in our jail and .... "

Interrupting, the Chief screamed, "Goddamnit, Ken! Who says he's the murderer? If I've told you once, I've told you a hundred times, I'm not convinced he's our man." The Chief's complexion was beet-red and it was difficult to tell if it was from the news the Mayor had just unloaded on him or because he was standing his ground regarding Strock's innocence.

"Not true, Lou. You said it yourself, you've got all the incriminating evidence needed to string this guy up. He's already admitted to being in the area those two nights."

"Christ, you just don't listen. Do you?" Lou was livid. "Strock only admitted that he was in Ralph Ames neighborhood the night Ralph was killed, but he didn't say he killed him. You can't convict a man for being *in the area*. And as far as the two kids are concerned, Strock says he was out by the lake that night. And you know what? Maybe I believe him."

"That's the trouble with you, Lou, you're too soft. You've got the guy in the palm of your hands and you can't close the deal. You'd make a rotten businessman, Lou. Well, that just doesn't cut it around here. We need action."

"So you're willing to convict an innocent man?"

"Innocent, my ass!" Koslo was also livid, his face red, his arms flailing. Barely able to contain himself, he screamed, "Lou, I want your badge and piece. Now!"

As he unsnapped his holster, Lou spat, "I wasn't aware that the election meant this much to you, Ken." Lou knew that Koslo was just a pawn for the local merchants who had been whipped into a frenzy, not only by the local newspaper, but by the Mayor's office as well. If he was more interested in getting at the truth than cow-towing to them, they'd be a lot better off.

"Are you sure you have the power to do this, Ken?"

Knitting his eyebrows, Koslo snapped, "Of course I have the power. I can suspend any town official who's derelict in his duties."

Upon hearing that, Lou reached his boiling point. He moved toward the Mayor, then thought better of it. He sat back down. Instead, he squeezed the arms of the chair tightly with his hands, trying in vain to quell his blood pressure and a churning stomach.

After several moments, he said, "What about the town council? Don't you need their approval?"

"Yes, they have the right to review my actions, and they will at the next council meeting. Of course, if they vote to reinstate you, then I'll be forced to do so, but I wouldn't count on that happening. The council has never voted against me." His look conveyed a certain self-righteousness.

Getz's first inclination was to bust Ken Koslo in the jaw, but he realized that that wouldn't solve much of anything. Instead, he removed his weapon and threw it *and* his badge down on the Mayor's desk. The five-pointed star hit the desk, then spun a couple of times before landing on the hardwood floor with a tinny clink. Both stared at it but neither offered to pick it up.

As he started to walk out of his office, he suddenly turned and faced the Mayor. "Who you got in mind as my replacement?"

"I'm going to ask Billy Chalk. Is that okay?" The Mayor's tone was now filled with remorse.

Lou said, "Yeah, Billy's a good man. You know you're going to be short handed for a while. You might want to check with the Sheriff's Department. Maybe they can temporarily assign a man to help Billy out." *And Koslo doesn't think I care about this town*, he groaned. *That sonofabitch.*

"Thanks, Lou. I'll ask Arnett if he can send somebody over."

Rather than slamming it, Lou quietly closed the office door. *Sheriff Harry Arnett. I'll be dipped.*

LOU GETZ DIDN'T bother to stop by the police station and explain what just happened. He probably should have but couldn't control his rage long enough to go in and tell the others what had happened. Hell, he wasn't sure himself what just went on. Anyway, he took the coward's way out and headed home instead. He would return the department vehicle in the morning.

He spent most of that evening on the telephone, first with Margaret who he called as soon as he walked through the door. At that moment, he needed a friend. While he declined her invitation for dinner — he was exhausted and didn't want his mood to influence her evening — he did avail himself of her soft voice and tender words that somehow made everything that had happened seem trivial. After talking for almost an hour, his feelings of shame, embarrassment and disappointment had diminished. No longer a bundle of nerves and in a somewhat more agreeable mood, he rationalized that things were not that important anymore. The fact that he had held his ground with the Mayor was comfort alone. *I swore to uphold the law and search for the truth, not to placate every greedy merchant by putting the wrong people behind bars,* he thought. Breakfast at Margaret's the following morning made it all that much sweeter.

Five minutes hadn't gone by when a frantic Billy Chalk called.

"I don't know what to do, Chief. I don't know what he expects me to do that you haven't done already. I told that to the Mayor and he told me not to worry about it."

"Billy, I can't tell you what to do. I can only tell you what I feel. There's a strong possibility that the Mayor is trying to pin these murders on the wrong man. To appease the townsfolk, he's looking for instant results. It's a vigilante mentality, I tell you. I think it's going to be disastrous once the truth comes out. Call it a hunch, but that's how I feel."

"What do you think I should do, Chief?"

"First off, stop calling me Chief. As of five o'clock this afternoon, I was relieved of my duties as Police Chief, at least temporarily." When he got no response, he continued. "Seriously, Billy, take the assignment, just don't let the Mayor run roughshod over you *or* the department. Keep at it, keep looking for evidence. It's out there somewhere. We just haven't found it yet. Call me at any hour if you have any questions. Okay?"

Billy hesitated and the Chief could almost feel his frustration through the phone. Billy felt sick, like Judas who betrayed Jesus for thirty pieces of silver. "Okay, I guess. Chief, when does the council meet again?"

"Not for another twenty-eight days, Billy. So do me proud. Who knows, maybe this is a blessing in disguise. I'm getting a little too old for this lawman bullshit anyhow. Oh, by the way, did the Mayor say anything about the Sheriff's Department assigning one of his men?"

"Yeah, Harry Arnett's sending over Karl Myers. I know him from bowling. He's a good man."

Lou Getz cradled the receiver and realized that his mood was turning dark again. Had he done all he could have to solve the rash of murders in Mauch Chunk? Heaven knew, he had botched the first investigation when he failed to comb the crime scene for evidence. A lawman shouldn't assume anything and, regrettably, he had assumed that the two kids were involved in some sort of weird suicide pact.

Was he being just as pig-headed about Clinton Strock and his possible involvement in the crimes? While he didn't think so, he could be wrong. Maybe he didn't press hard enough. Maybe the mayor was right. Maybe Lou Getz couldn't *close a deal*.

The Chief, or ex-Chief, fell asleep on his lounge chair sometime during the Texaco Star Theater. He awoke around two in the morning and shuffled off to the bedroom. For the first time in memory, he had skipped dinner. At some point during the day, he had lost his appetite and never regained it. There were too many things happening at once, most of them spinning out of control.

CHAPTER FOURTEEN

WHEN MAUCH CHUNK'S newest civilian, Louis Getz, awoke the following morning, he not only felt a new sense of freedom, but a splitting headache to boot, something he attributed to his confrontation with the Mayor the previous afternoon. The fact that he hadn't had dinner might have also been a contributing factor. Hell, there was so much swirling around in the dusty air, he wasn't sure what was going on.

His morning shower took longer than usual. He used the steam and pulsating water to help loosen his taut muscles, as well as ease some of the tension that had been building since his encounter with Koslo. He tried not to let it bother him. If in fact the Mayor was supported by those puppets on the town council and he was ultimately relieved of his duties as Chief of Police, so be it. Sixty years of age seemed like an appropriate time to pack it in. So why not? As Lou shook his head to shed some of his doubts as well as the excess water, Koslo's tone still stuck like a burr underneath his saddle.

He was drying himself off with a large bath towel when the first telephone call came in. Chick Devaney, a reporter from the Mauch Chunk Times-News, wanted the Chief's side of the firing. Lou politely told him that he had nothing to say and promptly hung up the phone. Devaney was an all-right guy, but Lou didn't want to dignify what had happened with any sort of statement, at least not yet.

The second call was from Harry Arnett, who agreed that the Mayor was a horse's ass and the townsfolk would realize it sooner rather than later. Arnett had quickly become one of Lou's closest allies.

The final call came in as Lou slipped on his very unofficial woolen trousers. He tripped and almost fell on his way to pick up the receiver.

"Lou," Harold shouted. "I just heard what happened. I'm really sorry. Koslo can be a bear sometimes, but I wouldn't worry about it. The town council will never back him."

Getz thanked Harold for his concern, but said that he wasn't sure that the council was that independent. "At the moment, Harold, I really don't give a hoot one way or the other. Actually, I'm relieved." He checked the clock on the night stand, then said, "Thanks for your concern, Harold, but I've got an appointment, so I .... "

Harold interrupted, "No wait, Lou. Don't hang up. I think I have something that may help you in your investigation of these hangings."

"It's no longer my investigation, Harold. Maybe you should talk with Billy Chalk. He's in charge now."

"Lou, this is important." His voice was strained. "When can we get together?"

Lou released a long sigh, then answered, "I suppose I could meet you for lunch."

"That's no good. I have to drive to Harrisburg later this morning. Can we meet now?" Harold pleaded.

Getz explained that he was heading out to Margaret Wenzel's in fifteen minutes. He supposed that he could meet Harold out there but he would have to check with Margaret first, to make sure it wouldn't be an imposition. Getz said he would let him know. *This better be important, Harold, very important,* Lou groaned.

Lou and Harold arrived out at the lake about the same time and Margaret opened her front door and greeted them both as they ambled up her front walk. Inside, Lou thought he smelled the remnants of the tear gas, but laughed when he realized that his mind was just playing tricks with him. What he most likely smelled was bacon sizzling away on the frying pan back in the kitchen. *Tear gas and bacon,* he thought. *I better get a grip.*

Although Lou had looked forward to spending time alone with Margaret, he knew that Harold was not one to trivialize. Whatever he had must be important.

As Margaret poured coffee, the boys eased their overweight bellies in at the kitchen table. "This is a whole lot nicer than sitting with those two nitwits down at the diner." Harold laughed.

Lou toyed with the idea of asking him why he *did* hang around with Roy and George, reconsidered, then when he could no longer stand it, said, "Okay, Harold, what's so darn important?" Margaret sat down next to Lou and they waited for Harold's big discovery.

Harold took a sip of coffee, cleared his throat, then began. "As a reporter for many years, I had to keep my eyes and ears open at all times just so I wouldn't miss out on an important story. A good reporter has the ability to be at the scene at about the same time a story breaks. I guess it's something a newspaperman never loses, that knack to smell out a good story."

"Get to the point, Harold." Getz had become frustrated. This was not how he envisioned his quiet morning with Margaret.

Embarrassed, Harold nodded, then continued. "Okay. What has happened to this town is terrible. That three of our own could be murdered for no apparent reason is beyond comprehension. That's when it hit me." Harold took a small bite of his scrambled egg and said, "It was the way they were killed that peaked my interest."

Lou placed his fork down on his plate, looked quizzingly at Margaret, then back at Harold. "I'm not following you, Harold."

Brandishing his fork like a man about to commit a crime himself, Harold said, "Think about it. What is this town's legacy?" Margaret and Lou offered no response.

"To this very day, the residents of this tiny coal-mining town live under a very dark cloud and it's not just the one caused by the coal dust." Harold looked at Margaret and Lou who both had blank expressions on their faces.

"Come on, you have to know what I'm referring to. Remember, way back in eighteen seventy-seven, four men were rushed to judgment, then later hanged for the deaths of two coal mining superintendents? Hanged is the operative word here, folks. Do you see what I'm driving at?"

Margaret and Lou both shook their heads.

Smiling sheepishly, Harold said, "Well, to tell you the truth, I didn't know at first, either. But then like any good reporter, I started to do some digging. Yesterday, I think I came up with the thread that will help sew this case up. Mind you, I don't have the 'who' yet, but I think I figured out the 'why'."

Their breakfast now cold and long forgotten, Lou and Margaret stared at Harold and hung on his every word as he set the scene.

Harold took them back to an era when the Pennsylvania coal industry flourished, labor was cheap, conditions were deplorable and workmen were expendable. The owners or operators of the mines completely dominated the small mining towns. They owned the miner's home and the store where the miner's wife traded. He was paid in scrip, good only for rent and for trade at the company store. Things were so bad that the miners often wound up owing the company store come the end of a grueling work week.

Anyway, according to Harold, on June 21, 1877, four men accused of being members of the organization called the Molly Maguires met violent deaths on the gallows inside the Carbon County Jail, just six years after it was built. One year later, on March 28, 1878, another suspected Molly was hanged. Spectators crowded the main cell block to witness these hangings and, while it should have been a somber occasion, it wound up being more of a circus-like atmosphere. The townspeople somehow forgot that the condemned were all God-fearing men; men with families who honestly thought they had done the right thing; men whose biggest crime might have been that they were Irish. Getting hold of a front row ticket inside the jail was more important than trying to understand the plight of the Molly Maguires. Mauch Chuck, perhaps all of Carbon County, had been riddled with guilt ever since.

What precipitated this series of hangings, so said Harold, were the deaths of two of the bosses. First, a mine superintendent was approached by four assailants on the night of December 2, 1872 and was shot dead by one of them. Later, the General Superintendent was gunned down at point blank range in September of 1875. To the Molly Maguires, these men represented the strong-willed bosses and colliery superintendents who carried out the policies of the Philadelphia and Reading Railroad, the evil operators of the local mine fields. A series of wage reductions and firings with no cause, coupled with horrendous working conditions, sparked the most militant labor demonstrations in 1877.

If one was to believe Harold, the Molly Maguires, a secret and eventual criminal society also known as the "Buckshots" and "Sleepers," used their power in labor disputes for the benefit of their members and terrorized the anthracite region of Pennsylvania from about 1865 until the sensational murder trials and hangings in 1877 and 1878. Several historians believe many of these men were accused of crimes and subsequently hanged simply because they were Irish. There was no proof they were guilty of the crime of murder, and circumstantial evidence, hearsay and innuendo were used to send these men to prison. Mock trials had succeeded in exonerating the accused men, but despite the outcome of these re-creations, the fact remained that a total of 28 were sent to the gallows in the late 1870's for crimes they may or may not have committed. To this very day, the descendants of these men felt the negative effects of these executions. So, too, did the residents of Mauch Chunk. It was their legacy, like it or not.

When Harold was through relating his story, he replaced his fork, put his hands in his lap and looked at the two of them with probing eyes. For the longest while, no one said anything. The eerie silence was like a thick fog over a busy harbor. Everyone waited for the loud crash.

Finally, Lou threw up his hands and said, "That's all very interesting, Harold, but I still don't see the connection." He turned toward Margaret and asked, "How about you? Do you know where he's going with this?"

"I'm sorry, Harold, I'm afraid I don't. Margaret almost sounded remorseful. "You're going over some pretty old ground. Maybe you better explain."

Harold sighed like a school teacher who wasn't getting his point across to a classroom filled with inattentive malcreants.

He reached for the knife again and said, "I know that Mauch Chunk's history and its struggles back in the late eighteen hundreds are old news around these parts, but I think there's a connection with what's happened here." Harold stood and began pacing back and forth across the yellow and blue speckled linoleum floor.

As the other two followed with their eyes, he continued. "Now, let me walk you through this slowly. This is where my investigative skills come into play and, to be honest with you, it gets a little complicated, even for me." Harold was also being his immodest self.

"I don't know how much you two know about genealogy." Harold waited for a response. When he received none, he went on. "Well, anyway, as a reporter for all those years, I had to learn to trace family backgrounds in order to complete some of my stories. It's a tedious process, one that takes a great deal of time, concentration and patience." Margaret and Lou both raised their eyebrows.

"Okay, okay, I'll get to the point. Genealogy is a means by which you can trace a family, either forward or backwards. I've used it a few times when searching for somebody's next of kin or looking for someone who might have had a motive like a member of the family who might be in line to inherit a large sum of money.

"Anyway, something bothered me about the rash of recent hangings and how they might be related to the hangings at the old jail seventy-five years ago."

Harold spent the next half hour or so going over his conclusions and the process by which he arrived at them. First, he wrote down the name of each deceased on a separate sheet of paper and, using what he called the "pedigree" method, traced backward the parents, grandparents and great-grandparent. His findings were both astounding and frightening.

His first subject was Ralph Ames — Harold chose Ralph for reasons he would explain later. When he had completed his research, he discovered that Ralph's grandfather was a man called John P. Ames.

"You see, I played a hunch," Harold said. "I knew the name Ames was a sad reminder of this town's past. That's why I decided to go back into Ralph's lineage, because of his last name."

When Lou and Margaret offered no reaction, Harold reminded them that John P. "Jack" Ames, Ralph's grandfather, was the General Superintendent of the coal mines who worked for the Philadelphia and Reading Railroad. He was the same man who was gunned down by one of the Molly Maguires in 1875.

Lou was stunned. He had known Ralph Ames ever since Ralph moved to Mauch Chunk more than 20 years ago, but had no idea that he was Jack Ames' grandson. Ralph never mentioned anything about it. Margaret was also astounded and, like Lou, had never thought anything about it.

Why Ralph kept this a secret was no mystery, though. According to Harold, Ralph was evidently embarrassed by the connection. If word had ever filtered down that he was related to Jack Ames, the miners would have laid down their picks and shovels and walked off the job, for sure.

Margaret quickly refilled everybody's cup, then sat back down and eagerly awaited the next installment of Harold's fascinating tale.

"I picked Ralph for my first subject strictly on a hunch. I've written a lot about the Molly Maguires over the years, probably hundreds of articles covering just about every aspect of their struggle with the owners. In my mind, three recent hangings in the span of one week was just too coincidental. Then I remembered Jack Ames and started to put the pieces together."

"Are you saying that Ralph Ames was hanged because his grandfather was shot almost seventy-five years ago?"

"Yeah, Lou, I am. I know it sounds preposterous, but hear me out."

After gathering his thoughts, Harold said that he then did a lineage project on Mary Jo Stevens. Here too, he was able to do a simple pedigree chart, only this time, the answer was found by tracing back her lineage on her mother's side. Ruth Stevens, whose maiden name was Randolph, was the granddaughter of Dora Parsons, the only daughter of Miller Parsons.

When neither offered a response, Harold threw his arms up into the air and screamed, "Miller Parsons, don't you get it? He was the mine superintendent killed by the Mollies back in 1872. What are the chances of that happening?"

Lou tented his fingers underneath his chin and thought for the longest time. When he had considered all that Harold had presented, he responded. "If what you say is true, you're telling us that we have some nut roaming around intent upon retribution."

"Yes, Lou, I think that's exactly what I'm saying."

"I don't know," uttered Lou despondently. "Why would someone scheme to kill the descendants of two men who were murdered eighty years ago by a bunch of thugs? And why would he kill Mary Jo instead of Ruth? The mother is closer in line to this guy Miller Parsons. Right?"

Margaret wriggled in her seat and started to respond to Lou's question even though she hadn't been asked for her contribution.

Oh, the heck with it, she thought. *Whether they like it or not, I'm now a part of it.* "Maybe the killer went there that night thinking Ruth would be home. When he discovered that both she and Tom were out for the evening, he decided to do the next best thing and kill her daughter."

If what Margaret said were true, then it meant that Ruth was still in danger. "God, I don't know about you two, but this whole thing is scaring the living hell out of me." Lou clasped his head in his generous hands and groaned. He then scratched his head although it didn't really itch. A lot was racing through his mind and he didn't know how to apply the brakes.

"I'm still confused. Why would someone kill the grandson and the great-granddaughter of two of the mine bosses?"

For the longest time, no one uttered a word. Finally, Harold said, "Well that's what I said before, Lou. Somebody's out for revenge. I just don't know who it is, yet."

It was nearly eleven when Harold stood and announced that he had to leave. He was heading over to Harrisburg to continue his genealogical research. So far, he had been unable to find a tie-in with Pete Koegel. When a simple pedigree search failed, he had done a descendancy chart, a comprehensive descent list, generation by generation. This chart included aunts, uncles, nieces and nephew and cousins. That, too, failed to link Pete with any of the players back in the 1870's. Harold now wanted to check out the land sale documents, wills and tax records. That would take forever, so he wanted to get over there as soon as possible.

As Harold closed the front door behind him, Lou sidled up to Margaret and gently grabbed her hand. "You know, you're pretty good at this investigation stuff. Maybe if I had had you on the force instead of the other two, I'd still have my job."

Margaret giggled like a school girl, then squeezed Lou's hand. "What Harold came up with *is* fascinating."

"Yeah, and scary too. There sure seems to be a tie, and I guess it's more than just a coincidence. It'll be interesting to see what he finds concerning Pete Koegel."

Since breakfast hadn't quite turned out the way she expected, Margaret offered lunch instead, and Lou accepted her kind invitation without the slightest hesitation. First, though, he had to call Billy to tell him to keep a close eye on Ruth Stevens since she may still be in danger. He didn't give Billy all the particulars, but then again, he didn't have to. Billy always trusted the Chief's instincts implicitly. It was a good thing, too, for had he been asked, Lou would have been unable to offer much that made sense. If Harold's theory was correct, the town's primary focus had shifted from Clinton Strock to some unknown madman hell bent on exacting revenge for something that happened nearly 75 years ago.

LATER THAT AFTERNOON, Clinton Strock was tossed back into Cell 17. For once, he didn't mouth off to the guards. In fact, he hadn't said a word to anyone for some time, in part because Strock realized from the moment he retained him, this attorney was an incompetent buffoon, more talk than substance.

He had been interrogated earlier by a new face, an Acting-Chief William Chalk, but he didn't open up to him either. Strock didn't even bother to ask what happened to Chief Getz. He just stared down at the gnarly old table and avoided eye contact altogether. What was the use? No one believed him anyway. The town needed to convict someone for the horrible crimes and Strock was just lucky enough to be the one chosen. *I learned a long time ago, little people like me don't mean a damn.*

He lay back on his bunk, laced his fingers behind his head and stared up at the mysterious smudge on the wall. No longer something to fear, the mark had oddly become his ally. At last, he had learned about it's true meaning. It was a symbol of struggle. Now, when sun's rays allowed, Strock had two things to focus on; the spider's plight and the handprint that now signified his own personal struggle.

According to the prison guard who told the story to Strock earlier that morning, before each of the hangings back in the 1870's, some of the accused men swore to their innocence. But one in particular expressed his innocence in an extraordinary way. To prove he was being wronged, he defiantly placed his hand on the concrete wall of his cell and proclaimed that the future existence of his handprint would be an eternal sign of his innocence and unjust execution. The very day following his death, his handprint appeared on the wall.

The handprint had been painted over many times but always reappeared. When the area was replastered and a new coat of paint applied, the grayish handprint eerily bled through. The guard who spoke with Strock, without authorization, mentioned that there was much more to the story, but it would have to wait. If he was ever caught commiserating with a prisoner, he would be severely reprimanded. If they knew that he had also slipped Strock a pencil and a sheet of paper, he would be summarily dismissed, no questions asked.

THE SPIDER'S SILKEN lair is carefully woven to catch unsuspecting prey. It's not much different from the life I've led the past few years, Strock thought. But, suddenly, everything's changed. No longer the predator, I've become the prey.

His life first began to collapse when his father died from Black Lung, then later, by a bitter divorce from a wife whom he loved so dearly. No longer willing or able to toil down in the bowels of the earth with the other poor miners, Strock began to weave his own web, a web of deceit. He set out on his dark and crooked ways, using his cunning to cheat the most unsuspecting of targets.

At first, it started with a series of scams simply to survive, then because he liked watching the suckers squirm. Later, he crossed some people who didn't appreciate being duped by some small-time con artist. These victims didn't bother with the police. No, they went gunning for him. That was one of the reasons Strock held up that jewelry store down in Allentown. He had intended to use the loot to buy an airline ticket to the west coast, to get as far away from Pennsylvania as possible. He figured they would never find him out there. As it turned out, though, Strock was apprehended instead and later placed in the Carbon County jail. His life had spiraled out of control and he had lost all hope of pulling out of his free fall. Since the town was convinced that he had committed the heinous crimes against three of its residents, perhaps he, too, would use the handprint to declare his own innocence.

Each night, when he heard the loud snores from inmates emanate from the adjacent cells, he quietly honed the edge of his belt buckle against the concrete wall beneath his bed.

IT WAS A cold, dark night as Randy raced along the same winding roads he always took when making the trip to the meeting up in Jewett. With only ten more miles to go, he had consumed close to a half a bottle of whiskey and was feeling the affects as the alcohol ran through his blood stream up into his brain like a torrential river.

Roadside trees and telephone poles shot out from nowhere, and the lights from oncoming traffic seared his brain with the ferocity of a white-hot poker. As other cars approached, he squinted, quickly pulled the steering wheel with a jerk, then squinted again. Thank God it was a clear night and the plows had cleared the roads of the icy snow that had fallen the previous day. Otherwise, he would have been a statistic for sure. As it was, he was driving with blurry vision by the time he swerved into the parking lot in front of the meeting hall.

Like the week before, he sidled next to Brendan Conley's brand-new Chrysler, his front bumper lightly tapping one of the railroad ties that lined the perimeter. Before he cut the ignition, he took one last swig, then tucked the bottle under the passenger seat so no one would spot it. The amber liquid burned a bit, but tasted good as it slid down a throat that had become raw from the cold autumn air. With some difficulty, he stepped out of the car and staggered up toward the main entrance.

As the front door flew open and slammed against the adjacent wall with a loud crash, everyone turned their heads to see Randy struggle to right himself. While he managed to regain his balance, everyone knew he was drunk. It was no big surprise. He often arrived drunk and although he had been reprimanded several times by the older members — they had even threatened to expel him — he persisted in his deviant ways nonetheless.

At Conley's insistence, Randy sat in the back row while the president of the division continued with the business at hand as though nothing had happened.

Conley leaned over and whispered, "What the hell's the matter with you? You're drunk."

"Bullshit," Randy slurred. "I had a couple of drinks on the way over. That's all." He hesitated, then turned toward Conley with a glazed-over look and mumbled, "What the fuck is it to you, anyway?" His raised voice caught the attention of those seated near them. Several wiggled uncomfortably in their chairs but said nothing. Some felt that Randy was a time-bomb ready to explode at any moment, and no one wanted to be around when that happened.

Finally, from across the aisle, an older gentleman with a shock of reddish-gray hair and bushy brows that practically covered his eyes, growled, "If you two can't be quiet, then I suggest you leave."

Randy responded with a vengeance. "Hey, Pops, why don't you go fuck yourself. I'll make as much fucking noise as .... " His unsteady voice trailed off when Conley grabbed Randy's arm, then tried to pull him up off the chair to get him out of the hall before he stirred up any more trouble. Randy's two hundred plus pounds were the only things that stopped him.

Randy looked at Conley, withdrew his arm, then almost apologetically, said, "All right, take it easy, Brendan. I'll shut up." With that, he closed his eyes and fell off to sleep. Only

Conley's well-aimed elbow into Randy's ribs now and again stopped Randy's loud snoring.

Fortunately for both Randy and Brendan, word soon came down that the division president's daughter-in-law had gone into labor, so this meeting of the Ancient Order of Hibernians was summarily adjourned. *Thank God,* thought Conley, *another few minutes and Randy would be curled up on the floor with his thumb in his mouth.*

Later, Conley woke Randy, then somehow managed to get him outside and into the passenger seat of Randy's car. He returned to the lodge and requisitioned four cups of black coffee. Although it was barely ten o'clock, Randy was in such sorry shape he needed some sort of stimulant to enable him to make the trip back home. Conley knew there was nothing worse than a wide-awake drunk but he wasn't about to drive him all they way down to Mauch Chunk at that time of the night.

Lodge coffee was said to be strong enough to remove paint and Randy soon regained some of his senses. Conley was thankful for he needed to go over the plans for the weekend, something that required Randy's full and immediate attention. If the two of them were to ever gain the respect of the elders within the Ancient Order of Hibernians, clear heads and clear thinking were needed. *It's now or never,* he thought.

CHAPTER FIFTEEN

AS WITH MARY Jo Stevens and Pete Koegel, the funeral for Tom Holmes was also held at St. Marks Church. Since practically every available lawman in the county showed up to honor their fallen comrade, traffic on the narrow streets of Mauch Chuck stood at a virtual standstill. As a consequence, the service didn't begin until almost eleven, nearly an hour later than scheduled.

It was not surprising that St. Marks was jammed. Tom Holmes was not only a good lawman but he was a good friend to many who came to pay their respects. Whether as a father, husband, mentor, fellow-lodge member, neighbor or just someone who crossed their paths, Tom left an indelible mark on the lives of each and every one who attended that morning.

Tom's wife and three grown children sat in the front pew and listened stoically as Reverend Duncan gave the encomium at the main altar fashioned from exquisite marble and brass. Each family member showed the same strength and resolve that Tom exhibited during his lifetime. They nodded and smiled quietly as the Reverend spoke of the good father, loving husband, caring friend, honest public servant and, most importantly, a man of God. A quieting hand on Dora's shoulder by one of her sons prevented her tears from turning into sobs.

"O God, whose mercies cannot be numbered; Accept our prayers on behalf of the soul of thy servant departed, and grant *him* an entrance into the land of light and joy, in the fellowship of thy saints; through Jesus Christ our Lord. *Amen.*"

There was an odd nervousness when Pennsylvania Governor John R. Gallup got up from his seat and slowly made his way toward the front of the church. The leather soles of his fancy shoes slapped loudly against the Minton tiles.

Gallup delivered the eulogy, a *generic* tribute to Tom that could have applied to almost any lawman, from any town, from almost any state. It didn't matter much what was said, though, for the family was honored that the Governor of the State of Pennsylvania would take time out of his busy schedule and drive all the way up from Harrisburg just to honor this humble lawman. Little did they know.

Lou and Margaret paid their respects, then later watched from the stone terrace as the black hearse and three limousines slowly made their way out of the back parking lot onto Race Street. As only proper, Tom Holmes was accorded full police honors including an escort of eleven motorcycled policemen. Lou squeezed Margaret's hand as the procession inched its way west and away from their view. From the tower high above, the twelve bells of the carillon peeled right on cue.

"HEY, DAISY, HONEY, what're the chances of me and George getting a refill," Roy Gessler hollered so that everyone in the Sunrise Diner could hear. It was nearly twelve-thirty and many of the mourners who had skipped the graveside ceremony had come in out of the numbing cold for a cup of hot coffee. It was so crowded that Daisy had to put Kelly on full-time coffee duty. Her only job for the next hour was to brew and pour coffee, nothing else.

"I'm sorry, Roy, you're going to have to wait your turn," Daisy shouted over the din as she raced back and forth holding two metal coffee pots. "Kelly, make another pot. Will you, hon?" she hollered.

"Christ Almighty, you'd think that these people would have better things to do. What the hell are they hanging around the diner for, anyway? I can't even get a goddamn cup of coffee. Matter of fact, I can't even hear myself think." Roy made a sour puss.

"Leave it alone, Roy," George admonished. "They just came from the funeral. All they want is something to warm them up and then they'll be on their way." George removed a fresh pack of Pall Malls, then unsealed the cellophane wrapper.

"You're not going to light up now with all these people crowded in here?" Roy spat as he fired a look at George. Despite Roy's protestations, George tapped out a cigarette and lit it with great fanfare. Roy muttered something nasty under his breath.

"That was something, the Governor showing up at the church to give the eulogy," remarked a well-dressed man standing adjacent to Roy's booth waiting to be seated. He was discussing the service with a young woman who had accompanied him into the diner.

Roy's ears perked up like a hound's. He leaned over the table and whispered, "George, did you hear that? The Governor came all the way up from the capital to attend Tom Holmes' funeral. Now that's something. Surprises me, though. I never much liked the guy."

"Who, Tom or Governor Gallup?"

"Gallup, you idiot. He's pushing to build a major highway clear across state. Do you know what that'll mean? Do you?"

"Progress?" George didn't want to tell Roy that Governor Gallup hadn't traveled from Harrisburg that morning at all, but had come down from Wilkes-Barre, a distance only thirty miles, not ninety. According to the local paper, the Governor had met with members of the Northeast Pennsylvania Industrial Development Commission the night before, something to do with offsetting the heavy unemployment in the region. He wanted new businesses to be fully operational by the time the new turnpike was completed. George sensed that if Roy knew that the Governor's appearance at Tom Holmes' funeral was just another political opportunity, it would have only added fodder to his already over-filled trough.

"You know what, George," Roy whispered, "that girl behind me is young enough to be this guy's daughter."

"God, give me strength," George groaned.

THE MOMENT HAROLD returned home from Harrisburg, he tried to reach Lou by phone. Naturally, he was unaware that Lou had asked Margaret out on a date.

At that very moment, as Harold listened with some annoyance to the phone on the other end continuously ring, Lou and Margaret were holding hands in the balcony of the Capitol Theater. They were supposed to be watching *Blowing Wild* with Gary Cooper and Barbara Stanwyck. From all the giggling, one might have thought it was a comedy.

CHAPTER SIXTEEN

"I TRIED TO reach you last night but I guess you were out," shouted Harold, loud enough that one might have thought he was using a tin can attached to a string instead of telephone.

"Stop screaming, Harold." As Lou rubbed the sleep out of his eyes, he checked his watch. "Can't whatever you have to say wait until later? For God's sake, it's not even seven o'clock yet. I'm a civilian now, Harold. Remember? I'm allowed to sleep in."

Harold apologized for the early call, then explained why he needed to get together with Lou right away in order to go over his latest findings. With some reluctance, Lou agreed to meet him at the diner in two hours.

As soon as Lou and Margaret entered the Sunrise Diner, sometime shortly after nine, Roy greeted them with a, "Well, well, look who's here. Long time, no see, Margaret. How've you been? Maybe I should ask how you both have been." His tone was sing-songy, almost provocative, like he somehow knew that the two of them had spent the prior evening together up in the balcony of the Capitol Theater.

Without waiting for a response, Roy continued. "Hey, Lou, *we* understand you had a little problem with the Mayor." He screamed it loudly enough so it could be heard by everyone at that end of the diner. While he was fairly certain that everyone in town knew that Lou had been relieved of his duties as Police Chief, Roy just wanted to make sure, rub it in a little. Upon hearing Roy use the term "we," George slid down in the booth and tried to disappear.

His try for anonymity failed when Lou asked, "And just exactly what did you *two* hear?"

"Not much. *We* understand that Billy's the new acting chief." The top of George's head was now barely visible over the table.

"As always, Roy, you're right on top of things. I think the Mayor named him acting-Chief sometime late Tuesday afternoon."

Roy moved his eyes between Lou and Margaret. "*We* also understand that you two were seen making the rounds last night." As soon as Roy let the words fly, he knew he had made a huge mistake. Lou's piercing glare confirmed his worst fears.

Without any hesitation, Lou said firmly, "How about you and me taking a little walk, Roy?" Roy's resistance was no match for Lou's powerful grip on his upper arm as he was hoisted to his feet.

As they departed, Lou looked back over his shoulder and said nonchalantly, "Margaret, why don't you get us a booth down at the other end of the diner. I'll be right back. I'm not too sure about old Roy here, though." He smiled mischievously.

Not five minutes had gone by when Lou pushed Roy up the concrete steps and back into the diner. He deposited Roy onto his vinyl seat and watched with some glee as he collapsed like a rag doll. He then strode down to the other end to join Margaret.

"Good God, Roy, you're whiter than a ghost." George stared at Roy who was splayed like a drunken horse. "What the hell did he say to you out there?"

His breathing labored, Roy tried to speak but could not utter anything audible. When George thought he heard Roy's feeble heart pounding, he realized it was only the sound of a pickax outside on Hazard Square. He laughed to himself, then decided to leave Roy alone for a while so he could regain at least part of his composure.

At the other end of the diner, Margaret, a bit ruffled, asked, "What did you say to him, Lou?"

"Nothing. By the time I got him out there, he was shaking so much, I figured I better leave him be. At that point, I think I was more scared than he was. I only brought him out there to tell him to mind his own business, not to beat him up." Lou laughed.

"How come? Nothing he says will ever hurt us."

"I know that, Margaret, but it was high time somebody put a muzzle on his big mouth. It's okay if it's about me or the job I was doing, but when he brought your name into it, well I just felt I had to do something. I'm sorry if I embarrassed you, Margaret."

"It's not that, Lou. To be honest, I'm rather flattered." Margaret reached across the booth and laid her hand on Lou's arm.

Suddenly, the diner door flew open as Harold rushed in, his collar turned up against the cold autumn air.

"Hey, Harold, over here. We saved you a seat." George shouted his directive as though he were in a bidding war.

Craning his neck to get a better view, Harold surveyed both ends of the diner. When he spotted Lou and Margaret, he looked back at George and said, "Thanks anyhow." Without explaining, he stepped away as George fumbled for words and Roy stared blankly at the Formica tabletop.

"Morning, you guys. Thanks for meeting me so early." Harold slid in next to Lou, then tilted his head back to take in the smell of bacon, home fries and coffee as Daisy prepared the morning fare. "God, I love the smell of a diner."

"What has you so worked up, Harold?"

Before responding, Harold first ordered French toast, a small orange juice and coffee from Kelly. After looking around for eavesdroppers, he whispered, "I came up empty. As far as I can determine, Pete's family moved here sometime during the 1920's from somewhere over in Delaware. There's virtually no way his family could have been involved with what happened in Carbon County in the 1800's."

Margaret threw her hands out, palms up, and said, "Did you ever think that maybe Pete was just an innocent victim?"

Kelly delivered Harold's breakfast, then asked if Lou and Margaret wanted anything. When they pushed their cups toward her, she refilled their coffees, then returned to her station behind the counter.

Harold's interest peaked. "Whaddaya mean innocent victim, Margaret?"

Margaret tented her fingers and responded, "See if this makes any sense. Let's suppose that it was late at night when the murderer arrived at the Stevens' house to kill Ruth. Let's also say he noticed that the Stevens' car was gone, or maybe he even rang the front doorbell. In either case, he realized that the person he was after wasn't there. So he decided to go for the next best thing, the daughter."

"But it doesn't explain why Pete was murdered," commented Harold.

"Maybe Pete just happened to be at the wrong place at the wrong time. He was a witness and had to eliminated."

Lou rested his chin on his hand and stared out the greasy diner window. As he viewed an outside world that appeared as cold and stark as Margaret's eerie script, he quietly remarked, "You know, if you're right about this, then this matter is a whole lot more serious than we ever thought." Lou looked dismayed.

"Why's that, Lou?" asked Harold.

Lou turned his head and looked each squarely in the eye and responded, "It's one thing to kill for a reason. It's quite another thing if it's indiscriminate."

Lou paused, more confused than before. After several moments, he asked, "So where do we go from here? Is it a revenge thing or do we have an indiscriminate killer on our hands?"

Harold ignored Lou and said, "I think I have to agree with Margaret. It seems that Pete might have been just an afterthought."

Lou sighed as he faced toward the window again. "That's a hell of a thing to have on your gravestone: 'Peter Koegel, just an afterthought.'"

As Daisy refilled their cups, Harold indicated that he was still confused about one thing. Who would want to murder the descendant of a *victim* of a crime?

Margaret's eyes suddenly brightened. "Maybe the killer is a descendant of one of the men sent to the gallows for killing either Ames or Parsons. Some its some sort of convoluted retribution thing."

Harold snapped his fingers and shouted, "That's it! "Damn, I've been looking at it from the wrong angle. Thanks, Margaret, you're a savior." He reached across the table and patted her arm.

After Harold swallowed the last bite of French toast, he said he was heading over to the newspaper to dig out some of his old articles on the Molly Maguires. He thought the answers could very well lie somewhere within their archives. His eyes glistened with anticipation.

"Are you driving over to Harrisburg?" asked Margaret.

"Yeah, tomorrow. Can't today. I've got another matter to attend to. Tomorrow, definitely." He paused, thought for a moment, then said, "You know, I could use some help down there. Digging through those old, dusty files is tedious work. With the three of us working on it, we could cut the time considerably. Whaddaya say? Are you two up for it?"

Margaret looked at Lou and nodded. "Well, I know I don't have much else to do."

Lou laughed, then said, "Why not?"

After settling the bill, Harold, Margaret and Lou waved good-bye to Daisy and headed for the exit. As Lou pulled open the glass door, he glanced down toward the far end and noticed Roy staring at the table, apparently still in a state of shock. George gave Lou a cursory nod as if to say, "Old Roy here will be all right."

Lou and Margaret headed hand-in-hand up the steep hill toward the Asa Packer Mansion, the town's display of Victorian Italianate architecture that overlooked Mauch Chunk's business district. While only steps away from downtown, they both felt like they had entered a whole new world, one without bustle and noise. As they reached the first wrought-iron bench, Margaret and Lou sat down and gazed at the snow-covered pine trees off in the distance.

After several silent moments, Margaret said, "Lou, I'm still not quite as convinced as Harold seems to be."

Margaret's intense green eyes glistened in the late morning sun and her freckled white skin was framed by her auburn hair, now lightly speckled with bits of gray and casually brushed back off her face. Lou knew how beautiful she was but, at that particular moment, she was the most glorious thing he had ever seen. He felt a stirring.

He swallowed hard and responded, "Me, too. I'm confused about a lot of things." After several moments, he reached for her hand and their eyes met. "Something has happened to me, Margaret."

"What do you mean, Lou?" She pursed her lips.

He tried to gather his thoughts. Prior to that moment, random snippets had flitted into his head, but he had always been too afraid to assemble them, fearing that they would fizzle out and disappear forever. Today was different, however. Today, he saw things more clearly. For reasons he could not explain, things were now laid out in an orderly manner and he was able to move forward without concern for the consequences.

"Something wonderful has come into my life, Margaret, something I never expected, never thought I deserved."

Without removing his eyes from hers, he continued, "Up until a couple of weeks ago, I saw myself as a man who was destined to live out his life alone. Then you came into my life." He swallowed hard as blood rushed to his head.

"You've rekindled feelings in me, some that were only memories, others that were gone and long forgotten. You've made me realize that life is more than just being, that there's so much more out there, moments that should be shared with others. Margaret, I want to experience them with you."

Margaret's eyes sparkled as she looked at Lou's eyes and lips.

"I don't know how else to say this, Margaret, other than to tell you that I'm falling in love with you." Lou was nervous, concerned with what she might say in return. He felt the perspiration freeze on the back of his thick neck.

Margaret blushed slightly but refused to release his eyes. As Lou was about to explode, she compressed her lips, then finally spoke.

"Lou, I know that what you just said took a lot of courage and I appreciate how you feel, what must be coursing through your heart and mind at this moment."

She took a deep breath before continuing. "After so many months, maybe even years, trying to reconcile the passing of our spouses, we finally came to terms with their deaths, reached some sort of closure, and we were finally at peace, or so we thought.

"But that's all it is, Lou, a certain easiness with who we are and how the rest of our lives will be played out. Having gone through what we have, we don't look for, nor expect, anything more. Most of our life as we know it is over and, as I said, we're content and at peace with ourselves. And then something like this happens.

"Lou, I've also felt differently these past few days." Margaret stopped. She grabbed Lou's hand with both of hers and said, "I think I'm falling in love with you, too." She leaned over and rested her head on Lou's chest. As she felt her heart beating louder and louder, a lone tear rolled down her cheek. It was a tear of joy.

When she gently placed her arms around his neck and tenderly kissed him, a shiver went through both of them. The sound of children's laughter soon interrupted their embrace.

"Do you think two old fogies like us can actually be in love?" asked Lou, noticing a group of school children who had just reached the top of the hill.

As she picked a loose thread off of Lou's coat, Margaret responded, "Age doesn't protect us from love, Lou, but to some extent, love can help protect us from age." Margaret smiled, kissed him again, then nuzzled her head deeper into his chest. They stayed that way for what seemed like forever.

CHAPTER SEVENTEEN

LOU AND MARGARET dined at the Hotel Switzerland the night before, then later ambled hand-in-hand up Broadway to Dugan's for an ice cream sundae, one they shared. They felt so decadent and young at heart, something neither had experienced in years.

The shrill ring of the telephone the following morning caused Lou to fall through the cloud he had floated on ever since he and Margaret kissed. He returned to earth with a resounding thud.

It was Harold. He told the Chief that he was ready to embark on the trip down to Harrisburg. There was an awful lot of work yet to do, but with the three of them working simultaneously on the genealogical charts, perhaps they could come to some sort of answer by day's end. He wasn't sure it could be accomplished, but it was worth a try. Lou agreed. He had to. There was no other choice.

The long ride out to Harrisburg was uneventful *and* agonizingly slow. Harold's top speed was 45 miles per hour and, on several occasions, he used his hand to block the glare of the sun so he could check the speedometer. *Forty-five, just right,* thought Harold.

After the three of them arrived in Harrisburg, they each scoffed down a cup of black coffee and a doughnut at a nearby shop, then headed for the State Museum and Archives building on Walnut Street.

Once inside this stately granite edifice buttressed by huge Doric columns, they grabbed hold of the ornate marble balusters and scaled the winding staircase that rose from the huge central rotunda and snaked upward to the reading rooms, exhibits and research areas. Every footstep clicked as it hit the inlaid tile step and each little sound echoed off the marbled walls like a Swiss yodel.

By the time they reached their destination on the fourth level, both Harold and Lou were panting like love-starved puppies. Margaret had passed them on the way up. As the boys dragged themselves up onto the landing, she smiled suggestively, then said in her best Mae West voice, "What's the matter, boys, was the climb too much or are you just glad to see me?" The boys tried to laugh but coughed instead.

Although the physical grandeur had been diminished over the years by the wear and tear, as well as the encroachments of cumbersome equipment like microfilm viewers and mimeograph machines, the expanse of long study tables and bookcases filled with thousands of volumes struck Margaret. For several moments, she just stood in awe.

Once they settled in, Harold took the list of the names he had compiled during his earlier research back at the newspaper. There were 20 such names, all Irish and all members of the Molly Maguires. Referring to the chart he had compiled for Mary Jo, he showed the others how to trace the lineage. Since the names of the men hanged at the gallows back in the 1870's were the *known* quantity, they would have to trace the chart forward in time rather than backward, opposite from the way he had traced Mary Jo's and Ralph's family.

When he felt they were ready, Harold tore off the two top pages from his legal pad and split the list of 20 names among them. It was almost 10:30 a.m. when they began their search. There was not a moment to spare.

"THIS HAS TO be a first, Babs. I don't think I've ever made it here before Roy." After she unlocked the glass door and they entered, George hung his heavy winter coat on the metal hook above the booth. "I'll bet he overslept."

Babs managed to smile, trying to reassure George that Roy was okay. But she thought otherwise.

George sat in the usual booth as Babs brewed her first pot of the day. There would be many more. As he ripped off the cellophane wrapper from his red pack of Pall Mall's and pulled out a cigarette with his lips, he looked perturbed. At his age, he didn't deal with change very well and Roy's absence this cold Saturday morning represented a major change.

For nearly forty-five minutes, George just stared out the window, smoking and slurping coffee, waiting for the first glimpse of his friend rounding the corner. He was on his fourth cigarette when Babs — who had begun to worry herself — finally suggested that he call Roy.

"Yeah, good idea. Maybe I should. He might have fallen, injured himself or something." George's voice got lost among the chit-chat from other early morning patrons who had entered the Sunrise Diner. Stubbing out his butt in the ashtray, he got up and walked over toward the entrance to the rest room. He inserted a nickel into the slot of the pay phone, then dialed Roy's number. After several rings, he hung up the receiver and returned to the booth carrying a forlorn look on his face.

"No answer. Maybe he's out doing errands. I'll try later." He sat back down, then tugged at the collar of his green and black flannel shirt that once fit snugly around his neck. Quietly, he cursed Roy.

Another hour passed before George got up and redialed the number. After five rings, a quiet voice, almost a whisper, said, "Yeah." George thought it seemed less surly than usual, almost meek.

"Roy, is that you? It's George, down at the diner. You've got us all worried sick. Babs is a little upset so she asked me to give you a call, make sure you're okay," he lied. Actually, George was the only one who was worried. The others could not have cared less. Roy was a loud-mouthed know-it-all, a purveyor of half-truths, a Gloomy Gus and an all-around thorn in their sides.

"I won't be at the diner today," Roy said. "I've got other things to do. I probably won't be in tomorrow, either. I don't know when I'll be in." The voice at the other end sounded weak and defeated. "

"Are you okay, Roy? You sound terrible."

"I'm fine," Roy spat. "Can't a man spend some time alone, for God's sake? I won't be coming in any more." George thought he heard Roy's voice break. "I've got to go, George. Maybe I'll see you around." There was a certain finality in his tone.

George returned to the booth and sat with his head resting on his hands. After a short while, it dawned on him. It was over.

It had ended, not with a bang, but with a whimper. The final meeting of the Sunrise Diner Roundtable had been held the day before without even the rap of a closing gavel. Never again would Roy, George and sometimes Harold gather at this Mauch Chunk fixture to exchange inane thoughts, gossip or barbs. It was the end of an era, the end of mornings — and afternoons — as they had come to know them.

"Was Roy at home?" Babs asked. She wore a look of concern.

"Naw, still no answer," he again lied. With that, he inserted a nickel in the Sceburg 200 Wall-o-matic juke box, heard the hollow clank as it engaged, and then listened as Guy Mitchell sang "Singing the Blues," a tune that pretty much reflected his feelings at that moment. As his eyes dropped to the table, he noticed for the first time that his yellow-brown nicotine-stained fingers clashed with his bluish fingernails, one of the late symptom of his disease. A lone tear formed, then slowly made it's way down his cheek. He made no effort to swipe it away and just continued to stare down at his hands.

When the song ended, he gathered his coat, then walked out the front door of the diner without even a wave or a good-bye to either Babs or Kelly. He stood on the concrete steps, lighted a Pall Mall and wondered what had happened. For the first time in ages, he wasn't sure where he would spend the rest of the day, much less his tomorrows. The only thing he was sure about was the profound sadness he felt inside.

He buttoned his coat, jammed his gloved hands into his pockets and began a slow walk up Broadway.

As Babs watched, she clucked her tongue and slowly shook her head back and forth.

AS HAROLD, LOU and Margaret raced through birth and death certificates, property records, wills, tax records and old newspapers converted onto microfilm, one common thread ran through the genealogical exercise. So far, at least, all the families of the Molly Maguire members who were arrested and ultimately hanged had been forced to leave the coal regions or continue to suffer indignities. Most returned to Ireland, others to as far away as Australia. Some even headed west. They all had one quest; to get as far away from the anthracite area as humanly possible. Without the support of either the Catholic Church or the Ancient Order of Hibernians, any semblance of a future in Carbon or Schuylkill Counties was virtually impossible for these impoverished folks.

By late morning, Harold finally discovered something. From all the evidence, the family of the man thought to have actually fired the bullet that killed Jack Ames was still in the area, some place near Jewett. Property records showed that in 1941, the family bought lot #7, block #57 located on St. Rose Place. The birth records indicated that they had one son. He jotted down the name and the son's last known address.

Nothing else registered with Harold, or any of them for that matter, until around three-thirty in the afternoon when Lou discovered that the descendants of Thomas Finnegan, the man who allegedly killed Miller Parsons, had lived nearby. This bit of news could not have come soon enough for all three were tired, hungry and just a tad irascible.

Although Thomas Finnegan's wife, daughter and two young boys returned to Ireland for good in 1881, their married daughter Brigitte returned to Hazelton, Pennsylvania in 1902 and remained there until 1949. Her name was removed from the tax rolls after that. Death records showed that Brigitte and her husband Patrick both died on June 19, 1949. According to the death certificates, both deaths were by asphyxiation and considered *suspicious in nature,* whatever that meant. What struck Lou the hardest was the last name on the pedigree chart, the name of Brigitte and Patrick's son.

Suddenly, Lou stood up abruptly, tipping his chair over in the process. "Oh, my God! I've got to find a phone." All the blood had drained from Lou's face.

Stunned, Margaret asked what was the matter.

Without responding, Lou ran out of the room as fellow-researchers throughout the room watched in dismay. He raced down the spiral stairs, two steps at a time, found a pay phone on the second floor, inserted a nickel and dialed police head-quarters down in Mauch Chunk.

"Annie, this is the Chief." In too much of hurry to worry about formalities or idle chitchat, he barked, "Let me speak to Billy."

When Annie said that Billy had gone out to his sister's place — his nephew had been rushed to the hospital — Lou asked her to do him a favor. He needed her to make some in-quiries regarding a family out in Jewett. Lou said that he would call back in an hour and hung up the receiver. He didn't like being so short with Annie, but time was definitely of the essence.

Lou raced back up the stairs to the fourth level and reen-tered the room much as he had left it, noisily and panting like a 15-year-old border collie.

"C'mon, you guys," he coughed. "We've got to get out of here. I'll explain in the car." Perspiration had dampened his collar.

They gathered up their material without chatting and de-parted, much to the delight of the others in the room who had not appreciated the disturbance.

They bounded down the stairs with Lou in the lead but stopped when they reached the main rotunda so Harold could catch his breath. He had lost it somewhere between the third and first levels. When his color returned, they flew out the main doors and back out onto the street.

"Are you going to tell us what's going on here, Lou?" Harold coughed as they raced to where the car was parked.

"As soon as we're in the car and on our way. C'mon, hurry!"

Since Harold was a bit poky on the road, Lou suggested that he take the wheel on the way back. Harold would have none of it. It was his car and he was going to drive and that was that. He had gotten them there and he would get them back. *But when?* Lou sighed.

It was after five by the time they left the Harrisburg city line and it would take at least two hours to reach Mauch Chunk, maybe longer with Harold at the helm.

Finally, Margaret demanded, "Okay, Lou, this has gone on long enough. What in tarnation is going on?"

Lou, who leaned against the passenger-side door, tried as best he could to explain who he thought was the murderer. The others were stunned and stared at him in disbelief. In fact, for the first time since they had left Harrisburg, Harold took his eyes off the road despite poor visibility and windy roads that led north back into Mauch Chunk. It was nearly six-thirty and the sun had long nestled behind the Blue Mountains.

At normal speeds, an automobile whooshed by the array of souvenir stands, campsites, motels and service stations that dotted the landscape. With Harold driving, though, the these same things seemed to be in slow motion.

Lou looked at Harold and asked him one more time to please step on it, that Ruth's life may hang in the balance.

Annoyed, Harold snapped, "I'm going as fast as I can, Lou."

"I know that, Harold, but is it as fast as the car can go?" When they came up on The Arrowhead Motel, Lou asked Harold to pull off so he could make another phone call. He slammed the car door, then raced toward the tiny office and located the pay phone. As he waited patiently for Annie to pick up, Lou noticed a man and a woman behind the reservation desk who appeared to be engaged in everything but motel business. Lou turned and focused on Harold's automobile instead. To reduce the numbing effect of the chilling wind, he retracted his head down into his heavy coat. "Annie, this is Chief Getz again. Did you have any luck?"

"I sure did." Annie told him what she had learned.

"Damn!" With his suspicions now confirmed, he felt an uneasiness in the pit of his stomach. With a hint of bile now in his throat, Lou said, "Who's watching the Stevens' house tonight?"

Annie responded, "No one, Chief. The Mayor told Billy to forget about it, that it was a waste of manpower. He said that they had their man locked up at the jail so there was no need for another wasteful expense the town couldn't afford. I'm sorry, Chief. I thought you knew about it."

Lou dropped the hand holding the receiver and rubbed his eyes with the other. He snatched the phone back up. "Annie, where's Randy?" He tried to control himself.

"He's off tonight, Chief Getz. With Billy over at his sisters, the only one out there tonight is the new guy the Sheriff's office loaned us."

"Get him on the two-way radio." the Chief ordered. "Tell him to go up to the Stevens' house and wait. We'll meet him there in forty-five minutes. Annie, call the Sheriff's Department, too. Tell them to send a second car up there right away."

"What is it, Chief Getz? What's going on?"

"I think that somebody is going to try and kill Ruth Stevens tonight." There was dead silence at the other end of the line.

Lou replaced the receiver and ran back to the car. As he entered through the passenger side door, he screamed, "C'mon, Harold. Hit it! We don't have a moment to lose." As a kaleidoscope of images flew by out of the corner of their eyes, images of death raced through Lou's mind and, even in Harold's frigid automobile, beads of sweat had somehow managed to form on his brow.

With every new hill, the sound of the automatic gears changing became louder and louder. At one point, the Lou thought he could take it no longer. "All right if I turn on the radio, Harold?"

CHAPTER EIGHTEEN

AS THE THREESOME sped east along Route 22 toward Mauch Chunk, the high beams from an oncoming car blinded Harold who slammed his foot on the brake and struggled to pull to the right. As he hit an icy patch, the car racked, then fishtailed. The rear-end was heading directly for the metal guardrail that stood between them and a one hundred foot drop to their death. Without thinking, Harold yanked the steering wheel to the right. Only his quick reaction and the firmer footing up beyond the ice prevented a serious accident that could have sent the three of them careening down onto the jagged rocks below. The same could not be said about the other car that raced by, swerving at the hands of an apparent drunk driver. His fate rested in God's hands.

"Crazy sonofabitch. He could have killed us all," Harold screamed, his breathing labored.

"On this stretch of road, he'll never make it at that speed," Lou said. "He had to be going 80."

"I hope he runs right into a goddamn tree. We could've been down there in that ravine, the damn bastard." Harold's heart was racing faster than the very car he damned.

"You don't mean that, Harold." Margaret was the coolest of the three since from her vantage point in the backseat, she had witnessed very little.

"Are you okay?" When Harold nodded, Lou leaned back and said, "Okay then, step on it."

As Harold groaned, Lou filled in the other two. "They've taken the surveillance off the Stevens' house. Ken Koslo felt it was a waste of the town's money since they already had their man locked away in the jail."

"What are we going to do once we get back into town, Lou?" Margaret inquired as she sat up and leaned over the front seat.

Lou thought for the longest time before responding. "We're going to head straight for Tom and Ruth's place. Hopefully, we won't be too late."

THE CARNAGE WAS gruesome. One of the bodies had been jettisoned through the windshield and, like a slaughtered lamb, lay in a bloody heap by the side of the road. Two other charred bodies lay inside the vehicle, unrecognizable, faces hard and black like grotesque masks worn at carnivals, bodies rendered like suet. The gas tank had exploded on impact and the flames had engulfed the automobile within moments of the crash.

Three unidentified persons were dead, as was the driver of the other vehicle, Ronny Tompkins, the chief mechanic at Sweeney's ESSO Station just outside of Allentown. It would literally take the coroner's office hours to piece this mess together. Since the inferno had pretty much melted everything, dental records would be needed to identify the bodies.

The sight of the blistered paint on the twisted steel carcasses looked like a marshmallow that had been held over the campfire too long. It's black outer crust flicked off to the touch. The smell was unmistakable and suffocating — petroleum, burnt rubber and the vile smell of death.

Within a half hour of the arrival of the first officer, there were two tow trucks, two ambulances and six patrol cars on the scene. Traffic was blocked in both directions and would be for at least another hour.

By the grace of God, Lou, Margaret and Harold had missed it — barely — and were fifteen minutes outside of Mauch Chunk when the deadly smash-up occurred.

IT WAS ALMOST eight o'clock by the time Harold turned onto South Street and pulled up to the curb, two houses down from the Stevens'.

"Cut the lights, Harold. I'm going to have a look around. You two wait here." Lou stepped out of the car and carefully closed the door.

Margaret rolled down the back window. "Be careful, Lou, you don't know what's out there." She reached out and placed her hand on Lou's arm. Real concern blanketed her face.

Lou nodded, then cut across the neighbor's lawn using two large maples as observation posts. From his vantage point east of the house, he saw a silhouette in Stevens' living room but, unfortunately, the window shade cloaked the individual's identity.

With blasts of white smoke puffing from his overtaxed lungs, he ran to the side of the house, took his position and waited. Finally, he heard Tom Stevens' voice. He had just asked Ruth if she would put the water on for tea. *Thank God,* Lou sighed, *we made it.*

He raced around to the front door and rang the doorbell. When Tom opened the door, Lou put his finger to his lips and rushed in without a word. He quickly closed the door behind him.

"Lou, what is it? What's the matter?" Tom Stevens appeared startled as he walked backward through the foyer, not once releasing his eyes from Lou's.

"Where's Ruth, Tom? I have to talk to you both."

"What is it, dear? What's all the commotion?" Ruth came out of the kitchen, wiping her damp hands on her apron. "Oh, hi, Lou." She checked her watch. "What brings you up here at this hour?" Her words were cordial but her look was not. *Why would the Chief of Police be visiting at this time of night?* she wondered.

Lou herded them into the kitchen and told them both to sit down. As they looked up with confused, almost fearful expressions, Lou told them what he had uncovered. It was imperative that they leave the house immediately.

"I can't believe it, Lou," Tom Stevens uttered. It was as though he had been hit with a baseball bat. All his thoughts were a jumbled mess, first Mary Jo and Pete, then Ralph, now this. Speechless, Ruth grabbed hold of Tom's arm as her eyes clouded up.

"Maybe I'm wrong, but those are my suspicions. In any event, I want you two out of here right now. I won't take no for an answer."

"But, Lou, I've got to gather up some of .... "

"Don't worry about all that now, Ruth. Margaret Wenzel and Harold Seward are out in the car." When Getz asked if they knew them, they both nodded. "They'll take you down to police headquarters. You can stay there until this whole mess is cleared up. The main thing is for you two to get away from here. I'd rather be safe than sorry. C'mon, we're wasting time."

As Ruth left the kitchen in search of her pocketbook, Lou grabbed Tom and pulled him to the side. Following a few brief words, Tom ran up the stairs. Moments later, he returned with a small package neatly wrapped in a red cloth and handed it to Lou. Ruth was unaware of the transfer.

Like robots, Ruth and Tom shuffled to the hall closet, put on their coats and exited the front door. Lou trailed closely behind. Margaret got out of the back seat. As she held the door open, she noticed how utterly bemused the two of them looked. These were awful times for both of them.

Lou leaned in and spoke to Harold who remained behind the wheel. "Listen to me carefully, Harold. Take Tom and Ruth down to headquarters and wait there until you hear from me. Okay? Lou turned toward Margaret and said, "Harold will drop you off at your house if you want."

Margaret grabbed Lou's arm and gently pulled him away from the others. When they were out of earshot, she asked, "What are you planning to do in there, Lou?"

"I'm going to sit and wait. If my hunch is right, someone will be paying them a visit tonight. And when he does, I'll be ready."

"It'll never work, Lou. They'll be expecting two people inside, not one."

When it dawned on him exactly what Margaret was suggesting, he emphatically stated, "No! No way, Margaret. Don't even think about it. This is much too dangerous."

Her jaw set firmly and her green eyes aimed straight at his, Margaret explained that to pull this off, the assailant had to think that both Tom and Ruth were home.

Lou grabbed her upper arms firmly and said, " I'll hear none of this, Margaret."

"Lou, I'm not leaving and that's final." She compressed her lips. Margaret was known for her resolve. Some even called it stubbornness. "All that talk yesterday wasn't idle chatter. Was it?" She regarded his face with as much calm as she could summon. "I love you, Lou, and I want us to be together even if it means that we're both in harm's way."

Suddenly, a car turned onto Fourth Street and slowly inched its way toward the group assembled at the curb. Lou's heart stopped. It was too late. There was no where to run. *How can I be sweating in this cold air?* he thought. When he saw the Sheriff's deputy behind the wheel, his heart began beating again, just barely.

Speaking to no one but himself, Lou sighed. "If that had been who I thought it was, we'd be .... " His voice trailed off.

He ran up to the car and spoke to the deputy in hushed tones. He then returned, opened the back door of Harold's car and asked Tom if there was room in his garage to hide the police car. Though confused, Tom nodded.

As the deputy turned into the driveway and headed back to the garage to secure the car, Lou looked down at Margaret. "See, you don't have to worry. Deputy Hogan's here. Now I've got backup."

Her intense eyes targeted his and did not flinch. Rather than arguing right there on the street, Lou acquiesced and said, "Oh, all right. You win. We'll do it your way. But I want you to stay upstairs, out of the way. No buts about it, Margaret. I'm not going to put your life on the line, damnit. Do you understand?"

Margaret gave Lou a coy smile, then squeezed his arm with her hand.

Lou leaned over and spoke through the driver's side window. "Harold, there's been a slight change. Margaret's going to stay here with me and the deputy. Take Ruth and Tom down to headquarters and wait there. I'll call you as soon as I can."

Harold nodded. "Be careful, Lou." With that, he turned on the ignition, then slowly inched away from the curb and down South Street as the white exhaust captured the light from the sodium-vapor lamps above. In the backseat, Ruth and Tom turned and looked back at Lou and Margaret through the rear window until the automobile turned left and disappeared on Center Street. Ruth's tears belied her dead eyes.

Once inside the Steven's home, Margaret set about her plan. In order to cast two images on the living room window shade, she strategically placed a lamp on a far table and tilted the shade ever so slightly. Anyone on the outside would just assume it was Tom and Ruth sitting on the sofa.

She then made her way to the kitchen, rummaged through the ice box and quickly made two ham sandwiches for the men. She'd lost her appetite hours ago. Margaret then lit the burner under the tea kettle. *Wheeeee!* She recoiled when the kettle suddenly whistled, then held her hand over her heart to stop it from jumping right out of her chest. Apparently, Ruth had just turned off the burner before leaving the house.

When Margaret returned to the living room, Lou was missing. Unbeknownst to her, he had gone down into the basement to secure the cellar door while the deputy checked out the rooms upstairs. The creaking of the stairs signaled Lou's return and she smiled.

Standing on the top landing, Margaret asked, "Do you really think something's going to happen tonight."

"I have no real way of knowing. I'm just playing a hunch, that's all." He leaned over and kissed Margaret to assure her that everything would be fine.

Before assuming his assigned place on the couch, Lou grabbed the small package Tom Stevens had retrieved from upstairs and walked back into the living room. He sat down, untied the cord and removed the red felt outer wrapping. A curious Margaret watched intently.

Suddenly, Margaret screamed, "My God, Lou! Where did you get that?" She recoiled in horror.

"It's Tom's. He bought it a week ago. After what happened to Mary Jo and Pete, he said he didn't feel comfortable in his own home." Lying on Lou's lap was a brand new, fully-loaded .32-caliber center-fire revolver.

After he placed it under one of the sofa cushions — he realized that the sight of the pistol had frightened her — he leaned over and grabbed half of his sandwich. His stomach growled though he wasn't sure if it was hunger or just bundled nerves.

With that, Deputy Hogan came bounding down the stairs. "Everything's secure, Chief Getz." He then screwed up his face and asked, "You got a plan?"

"Well, Margaret does, Deputy," Lou responded. "But I'm not sure you're going to like it."

A BLUE AUTOMOBILE rolled to a complete stop on Third Street, one block down. They would make the rest of the way on foot. They closed the car doors, careful not to make any unnecessary sounds. Then using the shrubbery for concealment, they stole their way toward their intended target.

Both men wore knit caps, blackened faces and field jackets over their heavily starched fatigues. The divisional insignia and name tags had been removed from both uniforms and one of them carried something bulky underneath his coat.

Once on the Stevens' property, one man cupped his hand to his mouth and whispered, "Go around to the other side of the house. See if you can spot anything. I'll check this side and meet you back here in five minutes."

They clenched hands, repeated the phrase, "Here's my mark of innocence," then split up, tiptoeing to reduce the noise their heavy military boots made in the crunchy snow.

"DO YOU HEAR something?" the Deputy whispered as he fumbled for his weapon. He presented an odd picture considering he was wearing a woman's wig and one of Ruth's housedresses over his uniform. He looked utterly ridiculous.

It was all Margaret's doing. She felt that anyone peering in the living room window would just assume that it was Tom and Ruth sitting on the couch. Since Margaret wasn't allowed to be a player — Lou was insistent — at least she could direct this little melodrama. Lou agreed to go through with it only if she promised to remain hidden upstairs, as far away from the impending peril as possible. Lou still didn't like the fact that Margaret was in the house, but when she set her mind on something, it was virtually impossible to change it.

At one point, when Margaret and the deputy were upstairs rummaging through Ruth's closet in search of just the right wardrobe, Lou climbed halfway up the stairs and asked why it was taking them so long. When the deputy appeared holding two dresses and asked which one the Chief preferred, Lou smirked and said he liked the blue one, it brought out the deputy's pretty blue eyes. When all three laughed, Lou realized that this bit of nonsense actually eased the tension that had been building like a runaway snowball since late afternoon.

"Yeah," the Chief said quietly. "Sounds like somebody's trying to break in through the basement door. Remember what I said before? We have to catch this guy in the act so just sit tight. Don't do anything until I tell you to. Everything will be okay."

If Lou's words were reassuring, his appearance was not. Perspiration beaded on his wide forehead and his breathing had again become labored. The more he tried to control it, the heavier it got. He squeezed his eyes shut. He was frightened but couldn't let on. He was the Chief — ex-Chief, anyway — and supposedly experienced in these matters. He had to show his resolve in front of this young buck. That was what he kept telling himself over and over again as his right hand clutched the pistol. Unfortunately, even his own words sounded hollow for, in reality, Lou had never faced anything like this during his tenure as Chief of Police.

When the basement door snapped open with a sharp "crack," Lou said mater-of-factly, "He's in." Lou was as ready as he would ever be. In fact, his demeanor suddenly changed from jittery to calm. At one point, he even looked over at the deputy's strange getup and snickered.

It was the sound of the assailant's first step on the bottom of the cellar stairs that changed everything and made Lou acutely aware of his surroundings. His senses were heightened, his nerve endings exposed and raw. His shirt felt heavy on his wide chest and the pistol felt like it weighed 50 pounds. His whole body ached.

The volume on the TV, which had been purposely turned low, suddenly blared, and the low-wattage bulb in the table lamp shone with the intensity of a prison spotlight. He squinted and then jumped slightly when the intruder began to scale the stairs. He had not remembered the red-flocked wallpaper being that loud, nor the colors in the rug so vibrant.

And why is the clock ticking with the ferocity of a jackhammer? he wondered.

The ascending footsteps became louder and louder, eventually reaching a crescendo like the German *Blitzkrieg* into Poland. *Could there be more than one?* Noises and images swirled in Lou's mind, evoking a grim picture of uniformed men marching through war-torn cobbled streets, leaving death and destruction in their wake. The shifting green, red and black patterns spun like a kaleidoscope until he couldn't take it any more. He was about to explode. If it weren't for one of the deputy's elbows into his side, God only knows what would have happened. With a start, Lou quickly came back to reality. Beads of sweat rolled down his face and his stomach churned like an old stern-wheeler.

Lou wrapped his finger around the trigger, pointed the weapon toward the hallway and listened as the doorknob slowly twisted open. He heard his heart pounding in his ears.

As the footsteps became louder, they looked at each other before returning their glances back toward the hall.

Now the deputy wondered, *Was there more than one?* His worst fears were confirmed when he heard the hushed exchange of words. Lou and Deputy Hogan braced as the footsteps neared, then stopped abruptly. No noise, nothing. No more footsteps, no creaking floor, no whispered words. Nothing.

Lou's finger tightened on the trigger, maybe too tight, he thought. What if the gun fires accidentally, sending a round into the far wall? What do we do then? When the deputy looked toward Lou, Lou put a finger to his lips as if to say, *Don't make a peep.*

Suddenly, two blurred bodies exploded into the room, the first one lunging toward the law officers. Lou flinched, then pulled the trigger twice, hitting the lead man in the shoulder and sending him reeling to the side, careening off a serving table, then smashing into the side of a chair. The other bullet hit the far wall, shattering a light fixture that exploded like a grenade, sending shards of glass everywhere. The noise was deafening. As the wounded man collapsed onto the carpet with a loud thud, the other held back, frozen in icy fear.

First looking down at his fallen comrade, then at Lou, the stunned intruder finally uttered, "What are you doing here?"

Perspiring, his heart pounding like a tamp, Lou cast a disdainful look at the adversary, one that would melt an iceberg. After he caught his breath *and* his thoughts, he responded, "Maybe I should be asking you the same question, but I think I already know the answer."

From her vantage point in the center hall, Margaret gasped, her jaw hung in disbelief. She stared directly into the eyes of Randy Furey.

THE EDGY YOUNG guard stopped outside Cell 17. It was midnight and time for his rounds. When he shone the light through the bars of the cell, he noticed that the beam of light bounced off the floor and hit the far wall. He quickly inserted the large flat key into the lock and turned it until the bolt disengaged with a loud clank. What he first thought to be vomit was something all together different. It was bright crimson. *Oh shit! Strock's not asleep, he's dead,* groaned the guard. Blood had drained onto the cold concrete floor and pooled into a sea of red from a slit wrist that hung limply over the side of the cot. As a cold shiver shot up his spine, the guard bent over and touched the wetness, just to make sure. It wasn't warm like he expected, but cold and sticky. Suddenly, his stomach racked and he retched, covering himself and the bed. His throat burned and the stench was suffocating. When he wiped his mouth with his hand, he unknowingly smeared blood onto his lips, giving him the appearance of one of those grotesque painted clown castings at a carnival.

"Stock's dead! Strock's dead!" he shouted at the top of his lungs as he raced along the cell block toward the stairs leading to the main level. The leather soles of his boots hit the cold concrete floor hard, like a horses hoof and just as loud. This sudden outburst alarmed the other two prisoners who rushed from their beds to their cell doors and tried to look through the tiny openings. It was impossible. The metal grid of the inner and outer bars prevented them from seeing anything other than the concrete floor. All they heard was the terror in the guard's plaintive cry.

Finally, two older guards returned with the younger one and entered Cell 17.

"Geez, who the hell threw up? He shone the flashlight at the frightened youngster. "Jesus, Duffy, you've got puke all over you. Christ, it smells like shit in here. I can hardly breathe." The sweet odor of blood mixed with the acrid stench of vomit almost caused the lieutenant to throw up himself. He removed his handkerchief and covered his nose and mouth.

"I'm sorry, Lieutenant," the young guard sniffled apologetically. "It's just that when I realized he was dead, all that blood spilled on the .... "

"Yeah, yeah, I know," the senior officer mumbled through the handkerchief as though he experienced that sort of thing every day.

The senior officer reached over and touched the body. Strock was indeed dead. His flesh had already taken on the waxy look. With his flashlight, the officer could see that Strock's blood covered half the cell floor.

The older guard ran his fingers over Strock's eyelids and closed them, forever. As he performed this final rite, he noticed a shiny metal object that had been kicked underneath the cot.

"How did that get under there, son?"

"I don't know, Lieutenant. I didn't see it before."

As the older man bent down to retrieve it, he snapped, "Well it didn't get there by itself." Under the scrutiny of the flashlight, he saw that it was Strock's belt buckle, then ran his thumb over the edge. He flinched slightly. "Well at least we know how he did it."

Spotting something out of the corner of his eye, the younger guard suddenly turned and yelled, "What's that?" He pointed to a piece of scrap paper that was wedged against the wall beside Strock's flaccid body.

The senior man snatched it up and, when he had gotten the gist of what the note read, he hollered, "Duffy, go get the warden. Hurry!" The young guard raced off, slipping slightly on the way out of the cell.

It was a Saturday night and, naturally, the warden was long gone. The fact of the matter was, the warden had left the jail sometime just before three, nearly five hours earlier than he should have.

"What should I do," screamed the young guard who was now at his wit's end.

Another guard, a gruff old geezer with an unkempt beard, told Duffy to call the mayor, then snickered when the young man actually put through the call.

It took almost an hour for Mayor Koslo to make it from his house to the jail, less than a mile away. As he exploded through the main gate, he snorted, "Goddamnit, where the hell's McBride?" Koslo was mad as a hornet. He didn't like having his weekends interrupted by bureaucratic bullshit, particularly something that wasn't even within his jurisdiction.

"Isn't McBride supposed to be here? Where the hell is he, anyway. Why the hell do I have to do everything around that goddamn town? This is his responsibility, not mine." After several moments, Mayor Koslo finally calmed down.

"Let me see the note." The young guard retrieved it and handed it to the Mayor who was now sitting behind the warden's desk wiping his forehead with his handkerchief. Koslo slowly unfolded the sheet of paper and read the words scribbled on both sides.

The Mayor smiled, then boldly stuck the sheet of paper into his shirt pocket. He felt vindicated. He had said all along that Strock was their man, but Lou Getz challenged him by saying it *had* to be somebody else. *Who's right now?* Koslo laughed to himself.

This piece of evidence substantiated everything he had suspected or done, including his decision to remove Lou Getz as Chief of the Mauch Chuck Police Department. He would now receive the full backing of the town council that would grant him the authority to search for a new police chief. Billy Chalk was a good guy, a good cop too, but he was Getz's man. No, a new police chief would have to be found and this one would be Koslo's man. As for the election, he was now a definite shoo-in.

"Do you want to see the body, Mr. Mayor?" asked the younger guard.

"No, I don't want to see the body, you idiot. Get a damn doctor over here right away. He'll know what to do."

"Where can I get a doctor at this hour, sir?" the boy asked tentatively.

"How the hell do I know, son? Just do it."

A LOUD GROAN exploded from the accomplice who lay on the Stevens' living room floor near the hallway. Dull, lifeless eyes stared up at the ceiling and blood from his mouth effused onto the Stevens' light-blue carpet.

"We've got to do something, Lou," Margaret pleaded. "He'll bleed to death."

As she moved toward the stricken man, Lou shouted, "Hold it right there, Margaret. I thought I told you to stay upstairs." She stopped mid-step.

Noting her look of consternation, his tone softened. "Why don't you go get a towel from the kitchen. Maybe if we apply some pressure, it'll stop the bleeding." He then looked over at Deputy Hogan and told him to go with Margaret and call downtown for help.

"And, deputy, while you're at it, why don't you take off that outfit. You look ridiculous." When both he and Margaret hesitated, Lou smiled and said, "Go on, I've got everything under control." He pointed the pistol at Randy.

While Lou didn't much care what happened to either of the assailants, he knew that Margaret was right. They had to try and keep the guy alive.

As the one remained splayed on the floor, writhing in pain, Lou looked Randy in the eye and asked, "Why, Randy? Why'd you and Conley have to kill all those people? I am right. Aren't I? This is Conley." Lou pointed to the floor with his pistol.

Randy kept silent while staring at his former boss with a look that conveyed a multitude of emotions. He was confused. He couldn't understand what the Chief was doing at the Stevens' house. He was embarrassed for being caught in the act and frustrated that he and Conley had not completed their mission.

But Randy knew that two professional warriors, both trained by the Army's elite Special Forces, would not be denied. They were not only smarter but mentally and physically tougher than the others. They were also better trained. Hell, they had been in tougher situations than this. One two-bit police chief with a toy pistol couldn't stop two fighting men like Furey and Conley. Under his breath, he said, "Here's my mark of innocence."

The long, uncomfortable silence was broken when Margaret and the Deputy came back into the living room. Over Lou's protestations, Margaret immediately knelt down and unzipped the fallen man's field jacket, then carefully unbuttoned his shirt.

"Oh, God, Lou." The bullet had not pierced the shoulder, as first thought, but had entered just above Conley's left breast. From the amount of blood already spilled, it could have very well punctured a pulmonary artery. Blood spurted like water from a leaky garden hose.

Margaret gently placed the two dish towels between his chest and shirt and applied light pressure. Too much, she felt, would cause irreparable damage. As she administered to him, she noticed a coiled piece of rope tucked underneath his jacket. She pulled it out and held it up for Lou to see. "I wonder what they planned to do with this?" A noose had already been fashioned.

Lou looked at Randy and sarcastically replied, "Yeah, I wonder. I think we have all the proof we need to convict these two."

"Lou, we've got to get him to a hospital right away. He's lost an awful lot of blood."

"What did they say downtown, Deputy?"

"Your dispatcher's sending an ambulance right away," said Hogan as Margaret placed a small pillow under Conley's head, then mopped his clammy forehead.

"And she said that the Sheriff wouldn't be able send another car. Apparently, there was a bad accident out on Route 22.

"Damn, I'll bet it was that car that nearly side-swiped us," Lou grunted. "I knew something like this would happen." Lou ignored the Deputy's questioning look.

"What are you going to do with him, Lou?" Margaret nodded toward Randy.

"I don't know." His finger remained firmly on the trigger.

Suddenly, like a corpse reaching up out of a grave, Conley grabbed Margaret's throat. As she let out a terrifying shriek, Conley's eyes became as red as the bloody incisors unsheathed by his snarling upper lip. He had the look of a mad dog.

Stunned at first, Lou got up and quickly ran to her aid. Seeing the opening, Randy lunged toward Lou who sensed something in his periphery. He swung his muscular arm backward. The .32-caliber pistol slammed flush against Randy's right temple with a loud crack. As blood spurted and his legs crumpled, he fell face-first to the carpet with a thunderous crash. Reacting quickly, the Deputy removed his handcuffs and placed them on Randy's wrists.

By now, Conley's limp hand had already fallen to the carpet. His lifeless eyes stared blankly and, when he opened his mouth, the only sound they heard was a visceral rattle, the ominous sound of death. After his head swung to the side and fell softly to the floor, a tiny flow of blood drained from the corner of his mouth.

Lou looked back at Randy who lie quietly, blood oozing from a gash to the side of the face. He was out cold. He immediately turned his attention back to Margaret and asked, "Are you all right?"

Rubbing her throat, she responded, "Yeah, I think so. But he's not. I think he's dead, Lou." She nodded toward Conley. "I don't think he'll be needing that ambulance after all." She looked at Randy and said, "He may, though."

They retreated to the sofa, plopped down and exhaled loudly. Lou placed his arm across Margaret's shoulder and drew her to him. He caressed her face with a gentle hand. Then, with one eye closed, the other on the Deputy who quickly looked away, Lou kissed her tenderly.

Holding her beautiful face in his hands, Lou said, "It's over, Margaret. I think it's finally over."

CHAPTER NINETEEN

"MY GOD, LOU, just because he's the great-grandson of Thomas Finnegan?" Margaret said as they waited in Lou's old office back at police headquarters. "Randy seemed like such a nice boy."

Despite what had transpired, Lou felt a certain loss. In some peculiar way, he considered Randy the son he never had. Though a loose cannon, Randy often sought Lou's counsel, which he gladly imparted. Sometimes, Lou felt he was making headway. Apparently, he was wrong. Many times, Lou had to sit him down and read him the riot act. Although Randy's lips said he understood, his eyes often told a different story.

"And I know that something went terribly wrong when he was down at Fort Bragg," Lou continued. Lou took a swig of coffee and mentioned that there was also a gap in Randy's military record that couldn't be explained. Lou knew that he had somehow gotten his fanny in a ringer, but when he tried to check it out with the authorities, he was always given a runaround. All they said was that Randy was a crack soldier.

Later, there were rumors that Randy was involved in a white supremacist group, that he had been implicated in the beatings of two black paratroopers, but nothing was ever substantiated. His records were sealed and, when Lou hinted around about it, Randy denied everything.

"I knew Randy had a demon dancing on his shoulder, but I always thought it was just the alcohol. Little did I know that a demon was ravaging his mind, too."

"Anyway, Harold's the one we should be thanking," Lou reflected, adding that when they had stopped at the motel on the way back from Harrisburg, he had called Annie to confirm that Brendan Conley was also a member of the Ancient Order of Hibernians, Division No. 3.

After the ambulance and the coroner's van arrived, Deputy Hogan drove Lou and Margaret back to the station house —

Lou promised not to say anything to anybody about Hogan's little masquerade back at the Stevens' house. Brendan Conley was pronounced dead at the scene and taken directly to the morgue, while Randy was carted off to the hospital where he received twelve stitches. He was later transported to the Carbon County Jail for incarceration. If they could locate a judge on a Sunday, he would be arraigned sometime later in the day.

Lou stood, stretched his arms and said, "Margaret, how about we get some breakfast over at the diner. Then, maybe, we can arrange to get you home? You must be exhausted."

"Funny thing is, Lou, I really don't feel that tired. I must be running on adrenaline or something. I'm sure it'll hit me later." Margaret took one last sip of her cold coffee, then followed Lou toward the office door.

As the two of them were about to leave the station house, the front door suddenly flew open as Ken Koslo stormed in waving a sheet of paper high over his head. He nearly bowled the two of them over.

Koslo had the look of a vindicated man. His smile mutated into a sneer. "It's just like I said, Lou, Strock was our man all along." There was an annoying smirk on his face, one that screamed, *I told you so.*

Already exhausted and now very annoyed, Lou demanded, "What the hell are you talking about, Ken?"

"Strock, that's who I'm talking about," Koslo shouted contemptuously. "Strock admitted to the killings. Here, I have his confession right here." He thrust the sheet of paper out in front of him and shook it in front of Lou's face.

Lou snatched the sheet of paper from Koslo's hand and took it over to the light. After he read it, he handed it to Margaret.

> To who it may concern,
> I didn't mean for it to end this way. If you had asked me 20 years ago if it was possible, I would have laughed in your face. Maybe that's my problem. Maybe I'm too arrogant, maybe it's why I stopped being good, why I ended up the way I did, sitting in this God-forsaken place, caged behind these bars like an animal.

The last few years have been tough and I guess that's the reason I ended up here. Now that I've lost everything (my father, my wife and kid, and my freedom) maybe it's time I did something good for a change.

I remember when my father used to take me to church when I was a kid. The priest used to talk about redemption, that in order to get God's blessings, we had to first confess our sins.

Maybe I should express my innocence like the others who spent time in Cell 17 way back. Maybe I should place my hand on the cold concrete wall and say that the handprint is an eternal sign of my innocence. The Mayor of this town comes in here every day saying that I killed them people and every day I say I didn't. Well, unlike them other guys who spent time in this cell, I'm ready to confess my sins. I'm tired of running. I pulled off that caper down in Allentown and, if it helps the Mayor and the town any, I want to confess to them murders, too. Yeah, I strung them up and I'm sorry. I just want to do something right before I go to meet my maker. Maybe by confessing to these murders, too, I can find redemption quicker. I seek God's forgiveness.

Clinton R. Strock

As Margaret handed the note back to Lou, incredulity blanketed her face. "This sounds more like a suicide note than a confession, Lou."

"It is," Koslo screamed. "He just killed himself over at the jail." Koslo was almost giddy.

Confused, Lou said, "You'd better explain, Ken."

Just as Koslo was about to open his mouth, Lou held up his palm and said, "Wait a minute, Ken, let's get Annie and Deputy Hogan over here." He winked at Margaret.

When the others gathered in the hall, Koslo explained what had happened earlier over at the jail. "Just like I've said all along, Strock murdered Mary Jo Stevens, Pete Koegel and Ralph Ames."

After a long pause, during which Lou gave Koslo an unreadable look, he began to laugh. Soon Margaret joined him. The others watched with a certain amusement.

His hackles up, Koslo screamed, "What are you two laughing at? What's so *goddamn* funny?"

Lou responded bitterly. "Three people have died, no, sorry, make that four. And you're right, there's nothing funny about that. What is funny is that you see Strock's note as an admission to the hangings. And from the look on your face, you seem to take great delight in the fact that another person is dead." Lou was just getting started.

"Listen to me, Ken and listen carefully. Strock didn't kill these people, damnit. Randy Furey and a friend of his did. It's a long story and I'm way too tired to go into it now. Maybe someone can fill you in tomorrow."

"But he says he did it right here," stammered the Mayor as he again shook the paper in front of Lou's face. "Right here! He said he did them." Now hysterical, he pointed to the note.

Lou snatched the sheet of paper out of Koslo's hand, then with his face no more than five inches from his, he snapped, "Ken, if you ever do that again, I'll lay you out right where you stand." Intimidated, the Mayor stepped back.

"Read the goddamn note, Ken. Try and understand what Strock was really trying to say, not what *you* want him to say." Lou grabbed Margaret's hand and whisked her toward the door.

His face beet red, steam blasting from his flared nostrils, Koslo screamed, "Hold it! Where do you think you're going?"

Lou looked back with disdain. "None of your goddamn business, Ken. I don't answer to you. You fired me. Remember?"

Lou opened the door, then looked back toward the Mayor. "You want to know another thing that's not very funny? Because of your incompetence, you pulled the surveillance off of the Stevens' house. Tom and Ruth could be dead right now, Ken, all because of you." He held his look on the Mayor for a long time. Finally, Koslo flinched and turned his head away.

Lou grabbed Margaret's hand and said, "C'mon, Margaret, let's go get that cup of coffee."

CHAPTER TWENTY

THEY SAY THAT time heals all wounds and, for most of the people in this sleepy town nestled in the bosom of the Lehigh Mountains, they were right. But for others, like Tom and Ruth Stevens, the pain may only subside and they will never see the world in quite the same way.

Not surprisingly, the Mauch Chunk town council met and recommended that Lou Getz be reinstated as Police Chief. What was surprising, however, was that Lou declined. After time away from the job, he decided that he just didn't need *or* want the job anymore. He was way too old and didn't want the responsibility any longer. Lou felt it was time for some new, younger blood and, accordingly, recommended Billy Chalk as permanent Police Chief. The Town Council would vote on it during its next scheduled meeting.

Lou had found something else to occupy his thoughts and time. Margaret Wenzel and Lou became an item in this small, mining village, and were enjoying every moment of it. These two inseparable souls were seen everywhere and, if truth be known, most of the townsfolk were as giddy as they were about their blooming love affair. In some strange way, their new life together symbolized the town's new beginning, a revitalization of mind and spirit.

One of the Town Council members recommended that a committee be formed to review the handling of the recent events in order to determine Ken Koslo's competence as Mayor of Mauch Chunk. Yes, Koslo had been reelected as the Mayor of Mauch Chunk but word had already leaked out that he had made some decisions that had put the town at serious risk. The council would make their recommendations in one month's time, during a special meeting. Ken Koslo, ever obstinate, vowed to fight to the bitter end, but those in the know said he best hire a battery of lawyers because things didn't look very favorable for a long-term political career.

SEEMINGLY UNASHAMED OF the crimes he and Conley had committed, an unrepentant Randy Furey eventually confessed to the heinous murders with little or no remorse. He explained that they had set out to avenge the deaths of their forbears who were wrongly executed for the murders of the Philadelphia and Reading Railroad mine bosses.

He said that when he first met Conley down at Fort Bragg and learned of their families' history with the Molly Maguires, they had a running feud as to which of their grandfathers had actually placed his hand on the wall of Cell 17 to declare his innocence. While most history books said it was Conley's handprint, stories told by long-time residents of Carbon County claim the handprint actually was the mark of Randy's grandfather, Thomas Finnegan. Rather than continue their feud, they vowed to avenge the wrongful deaths of their grandfathers. Somehow, these two men had become totally disconnected with society.

From his Carbon County jail cell, Randy kept repeating, "Here's my mark of innocence." Understandably, Randy was not placed into Cell 17 like his grandfather. In fact, the authorities decided that from that day forward, never again would anyone be incarcerated in Cell 17. The cell was indeed haunted. Its legacy was just too powerful.

Randy also confessed to an act of terrorism, admitting that he had planted the bomb at the offices of the Pinkerton Detective Agency down in Allentown. He mentioned that James Dunleavy, the Pinkerton agent, was hired by the mine owners in 1876 to infiltrate the Molly Maguires. His testimony, which was mostly based on circumstantial evidence, led to the convictions of twenty men, including Finnegan and Conley, who were later executed on the gallows in the Carbon County Jail.

Randy expressed some remorse that the lone casualty of that bombing in Allentown was Dooley Ryan, an Irishman, but went on to say that the Pinkerton people were the detectives for the rich. They, too, were evil and had to pay.

Lou made one trip up to the jail to visit Randy to try and understand why he felt they had to avenge something that happened so long ago.

"You'd never understand, Chief. It's just something I had to do. My people were executed for crimes they didn't commit and, because of it, I sought retribution."

Lou groaned, *My people? Shit! What's he talking about?*

He placed his hand on his chin and calmly said, I'm confused, Randy. What I can't understand is why you felt you had to burn down your own house?" The Chief had just entered uncharted seas and didn't know what where the choppy waters would take him.

Showing little emotion, Randy replied, "I had to, Chief. See, they just didn't understand what I was going through, all the pressure I was under."

"What pressure, Randy? What were you feeling at the time?"

"Pressure to clean up this country, you know, get rid of all the people who don't belong here."

"Like who, Randy?"

"My parents just didn't understand. They blamed it on the Army, said that they were filling my head with hatred. My parents thought I was crazy, said I needed help. Well I guess I showed them." He smiled sardonically.

"Yeah, I guess you did," Lou replied. "Death has a way of doing that. It was such a violent death, though, you burning down their house with them in it." Randy didn't respond.

Lou walked away from their visit saddened by Randy's dedication to righting those long-forgotten wrongs. He couldn't understand who had laid this heavy burden on Randy's shoulders. Like Hercules at the court of King Eurystheus who demanded of him 12 labors, was Randy seeking purification for all descendants of the Molly Maguires? Or was it merely an excuse to kill, something Randy had learned to do — and liked doing — ever since his days down at Fort Bragg? Or was it that Randy just couldn't tolerate anyone who was different, anything that didn't fit neatly into his little, screwed-up world?

And was the Army partly to blame? Randy mentioned something about a renegade element that existed within the command at Fort Bragg that taught that war was not subject to any rules. If a comrade was wounded or killed, then a soldier had the duty to kill anyone and everyone who might have been involved — man, woman or child. It was the "eye for an eye, tooth for a tooth" mentality, justified because it was in the Bible. It was during his time at Fort Bragg that Randy learned to hate, hate anything that he didn't understand. There, he learned about annihilation, not assimilation.

There was no easy answer. Randy's actions were most likely the culmination of many years, and a combination of many forces, not the least of which was a childhood filled with gory tales that portrayed the wretched owners as monsters who brutalized the coal miners.

One footnote; just as they did 77 years ago, the Ancient Order of Hibernians was forced to send out letters to all divisions, castigating the actions of two crazed mavericks who in no way represented the thinking of the Order. History tended to repeat itself.

DESPITE ALL THESE messy matters, in time, the rest of the world moved forward. The town received a telegram from the widow of Jim Thorpe expressing both "delight" and "happiness" with Mauch Chunk's proposal to change its name to Jim Thorpe, Pennsylvania. The text of Mrs. Thorpe's telegram read:

> Story in Tulsa World here delights and brings great happiness. God bless all you sweet wonderful people there. Leaving tomorrow via Memphis. Will see you in a few days to discuss details.
>
> Most Cordially
> Patricia G. Thorpe

NOT ALL THE townsfolk were as excited as the Widow Thorpe. Cynic Roy Gessler bemoaned the town's decision and vowed to move south just as soon as he was able. Of course, everyone knew that he would never leave.

"Roy, you're a permanent fixture around these parts, just like that Thorpe twenty-ton granite mausoleum is going to be years from now. You're not going anywhere."

"Don't be too sure about that, George. I'm thinking about putting my house on the market."

"Thinking is a whole lot different than doing, Roy." George tapped out yet another Pall Mall, then lit up. He had a satisfied look as smoke billowed out of his nose. Suddenly, he began choking and, while Roy ignored him, it lasted for nearly a minute.

While Roy's return to the Sunrise Diner thrilled George no end — he'd been dragging his chin along Broadway ever since Roy's sudden departure — others weren't nearly as excited.

"Hey, Harold. C'mon over and sit here with us." Once more, Roy's high arching wave beckoned Harold Seward as he entered the Sunrise Diner.

"No thanks, Roy. I think I'll just grab a bite at the counter, then be on my way. Thanks anyhow."

Harold had more important things to do, like writing the biggest story of his life, the story of Mauch Chunk and its terrible legacy. He hadn't yet named the article, but his working title was, *The Sunrise Diner*.

The End

9 781575 322575